Steve Braker

African Paradise

A William Brody Action Thriller

Table of Contents

Chapter One	1
Chapter Two	25
Chapter Three	63
Chapter Four	93
Chapter Five	107
Chapter Six	129
Chapter Seven	159
Chapter Eight	179
Chapter Nine	193
Chapter Ten	211
Chapter Eleven	231
Epilogue	239
Book Previews	249
Copyright	259

Foreword

Dear Reader,

This is the third in the series of William Brody African Ocean Adventures.

This book is loosely based on the terrorist plot in 2002 to blow up the Paradise Hotel on the Kenyan Coast. You can google the Paradise Hotel Bombing to get more information.

I do follow the lines of who the perpetrators were, there are many conspiracy theories on the web relating to who was responsible. Living in East Africa, you soon learn that we never know what is going on or why. The story is interesting as it was one of the first combined attacks allegedly using the Palestinian Liberation Army along with the Al-Shabab. To me, this seems most likely, but the whole story is open to interpretation, which I have done.

The book is fiction, I know and researched the story and was living very close to the explosion when it happened. African Paradise is set in the same period as the explosion and the same area, all the other aspects of the story are fictitious.

I lived in Mtwappa for many years watching it grow from a sleepy, dusty suburb of Mombasa into a vibrant independent roadside town, over a period of about ten years or so. The place opened up as the civil wars in Somalia and South Sudan became quiet enough to start trading again. I have always had a soft spot for this growing town, and I hope that comes across in my writing.

The Full Moon Bar is based on a bar I know on the outskirts of Mombasa. It is still there today and largely as I depict it. If you are ever in Kenya on the coast then I would recommend a trip to La Marina Bar in Mtwappa.

Getting these stories out is enjoyable, but sometimes you really need a push and a helping hand. My brother Daniel helped me considerably on this one, I really appreciate his patience and discussions on what sounded right and what should be left out.

I hope you enjoy the read, let me know, my email is stevefreelancewriter@gmail.com.

Yours,

Steve Braker.

East African Coast

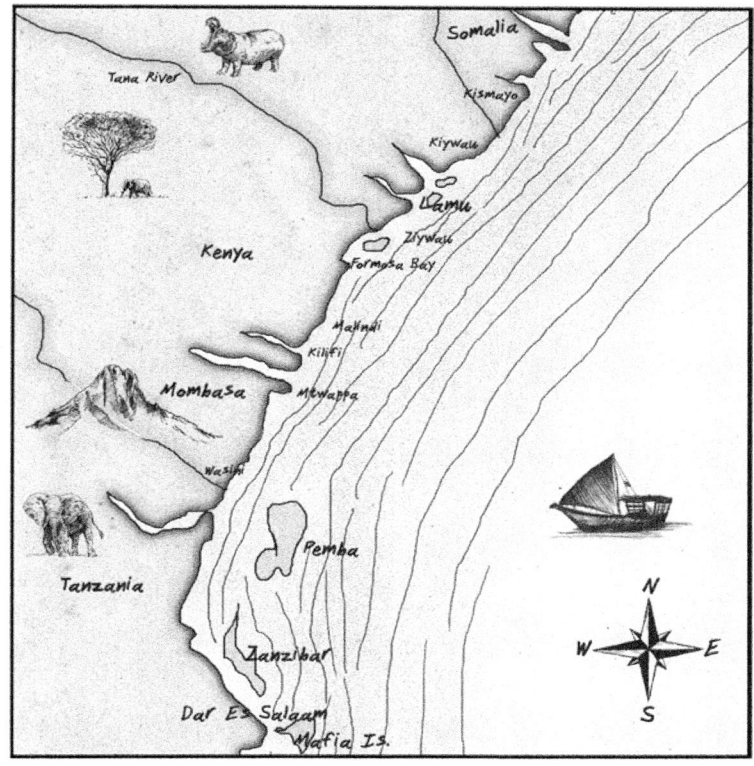

Cover art by J Caleb @ jcalebdesign.com

Chapter One

The punch landed, not a killer punch just a glancing blow. But it was enough to send him sailing through the air like a rag doll thrown by a petulant child. He landed on a small table that disintegrated with the force of his impact. He rolled instinctively and jumped to his feet, flicking some more of the rickety furniture at his attackers, gaining a few seconds. In the time it takes to get punched in the jaw and fly across the room, he had turned from an affable drunk to a killing machine. The afternoon's alcohol washed from his body as adrenaline flooded in.

He stood six feet from his two attackers. Thugs of men, covered in tattoos. Probably off one of the ships from the port. Both had large, bald heads covered in sweat, and were six foot plus and built like proverbial outhouses. This was a game, just a continuation of the drinking day.

Brody assessed his situation: first, escape. There was none, he was cornered. Second, attackers. They were big, but not in their prime, probably ten years past at least. Third, repercussions. Kill them and he was in trouble. This was Africa. He would disappear into Shimo-La-Tewa the local jail. It was like a Vietnamese prisoner of war camp. The poor, skinny, dejected men in chain gangs heading out to the fields to work in the boiling sun. Their keepers with pump-action shotguns and itchy fingers, ever watchful, looking for some sport. It was not a pleasant place to be in, and you never came out!

Brody ducked as a chair sailed over his head, smashing against the bare cinder block wall behind him. The two guys were ready to start the fun. The largest one broke into a merciless smile. He shouted, in Russian, to his brother in arms, "We'll have some fun with this white rabbit when we catch him."

His Slavic partner smiled in agreement, exposing nicotine-stained teeth below his twisted and broken nose. "You start, I'll finish this beer. Leave some for me."

The man-mountain had his blood up, that and a considerable amount of vodka. He advanced on Brody, kicking the lightweight furniture left and right. The other patrons retreated, enjoying the afternoon entertainment. The thugs usually used intimidation to make their opponents piss their pants. It was fun. Showing off. A bar brawl where you were guaranteed to win. The tourists were easy bait. If one dared to stand up to them, then a few punches and they were crying on the floor shitting their pants.

The young, brown-haired guy in front of him looked fitter than his usual prey and was not begging yet. But it would come in a few moments.

Brody had a split second to think. He would have to incapacitate this big Russian, and his friend. Then make good his escape as quickly and expediently as possible. If the cops arrived, it would be a whole different problem. This place was corrupt, the police were worse than the criminals. The cops would beat him to a pulp and chuck him in the street with empty pockets.

The fat Russian, stinking of stale sweat and burnt meat, threw a huge roundhouse punch. It had enough force to go through the cinder block wall behind him. The intoxicated guy was fighting like all Russian's Brody had fought, using volume rather than finesse. These guys just kept going and going, like a train on an incline with no brakes. Brody's training kicked in. He ducked. The punch cruised slowly over his head.

The guy in front of Brody was not solid muscle anymore. He had been once, and probably a formidable foe. But that was a long time ago. Now, although he was imposing, there was a spare tire around his waist. His tattooed biceps, up close, hung more loosely below his arm than above. Like the old ladies on the beach still sunning themselves when gravity had won the day. Trying not to hurt these guys was going to be tough.

The Russian spun around, then came back with a left. This time more of a haymaker, just throwing the punch in the general direction. But he was getting closer, and Brody was in a tight corner and would have to do something before he got hurt. All it took was one lucky shot. Then the Russians would have their fun and finish him off, maybe for good.

Earlier that day, Brody had been sat quietly at a roadside bar in a small town just north of Mombasa Island. Arriving a few days earlier, he had spent the time on *Shukran*, his lovely wooden dhow, moored in the creek below them. When boredom set in, the town had looked like a great way to explore, and an ideal opportunity to get to know the place. The constant stream of heavy trucks passed just feet away from the narrow path that served as the pavement. Life was everywhere, the town was hot, busy, and very dusty. He had wandered into a local bar just off the main strip. The place was a typical drinking establishment for this area.

The floor was packed earth, the walls bare cinder block, and the roof was made from palm fronds. Dried, trimmed, and stacked by old ladies in the village and called 'Makuti.' The roof framework was made of an interconnecting set of wooden poles, which looked like a massive spider's web above them. The ends of the rectangular building were rounded off to allow the 'Makuti' to sit correctly, providing a waterproof cover.

The highest point of the roof was some 25 feet above the heads of the busy drinkers. The whole thing was held up by a large tree trunk some eighteen inches in diameter which went from the floor to the topmost pole. The bar in the far corner consisted of more cinderblocks and cement with rough planks nailed to the top. A large metal grill stretched across it, with small serving hatches in front. Brody guessed security was a bit of an issue late at night. They sold warm or cold beer whatever your preference. The cold beer was more expensive as it was cold! African men enjoyed their warm sodas and beers, a quirk of the culture. Brody, brought up in the center of London, found drinking warm lager pretty much the worst thing he could think of. Especially in 100 degrees' heat with about 85% humidity. He paid the extra ten shillings for an ice-cold Tusker.

Brody was sitting enjoying the first beer of the day at a table not designed for comfort. The lightweight rickety structure was made from what looked like wood from the dumpster out back, with bottle caps under the uneven legs to stop glasses falling on the floor. Watching life pass by. After about thirty minutes, he noticed a long-legged, dark-skinned beauty wander self-consciously into the bar. She looked lost, like someone waiting for a friend, not sure whether to sit or stand or leave. The long-legged beauty really did look upset and unsure of her surroundings. A damsel in distress, staring at the road and the cars passing by as if expecting the right car to pull up with all her friends. Coming into the seedy bar, then exiting. Only to return a few minutes later with a very confused look on her beautiful face. She caught Brody's eye, "*Bloody hell my lucks in,*" he thought, and grinned shyly back at her.

Then, with the most beautiful bright white smile he had ever seen, the young lady approached the table and said, "Hi, I am a little lost right now. I'm waiting for my friends; would you mind if I sat and waited with you."

Brody stumbled on his words. He was not that good with women, especially not beautiful women who approached him!

"I'm Brody. I'm just visiting, having a quiet drink, seeing the sights of this lovely town," He said in his most honorable voice but with a hint of sarcasm.

The young lady replied with that sweet smile, "Me too. I'm on holiday from Nairobi. I don't know this area, my friends said to meet here. We are from the university they should arrive in a couple of minutes."

Brody just sat staring at her, lost for words.

She asked, "Do you mind me taking a seat?"

Brody felt his cheeks redden, then jumped to his feet like a twelve-year-old boy finding himself in front of the school head cheerleader. He grabbed a chair from a nearby table.

She held out her hand, "My name is Maria. This place seems rough. I don't know if I should wait here."

He quickly replied, not wanting her to leave now, "Don't worry, as long as you're with me you'll be safe."

She was right. The place was more like the Wild West in the 1840s than the twentieth century. It was called Mtwappa and was a growing town that looked after the large trucking community of drivers taking their rigs from Mombasa Port to Somalia and the Sudan. The frontier town was rough, noisy, and very dusty. Every walk of life rubbed shoulders in the rubbish-strewn streets from beggars to millionaires. You could buy anything you wanted in the twenty-four-hour markets. If they didn't have it now, they would in twenty minutes, just sit, have a beer and wait.

Maria was an excellent conversationalist, after a few drinks Brody was telling her his life story. With a quick, witty smile, she was obviously intelligent and seemed to know the world around her. She looked to be in her late twenties, with long curly black hair, liquid brown eyes that were quick to crinkle as she smiled. Her slender, toned legs went on forever. She was wearing a short jeans skirt which Brody would never have allowed his daughter to wear, if he had one. A tight, bright white T-Shirt covering her ample breasts. All in all, an absolutely stunning package. Maria sat sipping her drink innocently, but she seemed to finish at the same time Brody did, ready for a refill. As the hot afternoon wore on, he started feeling a bit light-headed. Maria did not appear to notice, chatting easily with him. It seemed to Brody that he was the centre of her world. Everything else merged into the background like it didn't exist. Her attention focused on nothing else, she hung on every word he said, smiling and nodding encouraging him to talk. It was like talking to a therapist. Everything was OK, the story was all about him. The time flew by. Glancing at his watch, he noticed that two hours had passed and Maria had her hand on his leg. Brody thought, in his semi-intoxicated state, *"Well I'm the best-looking guy here what the hell this place is getting better and better."*

Then the proverbial shit hit the fan when two huge guys walked into the bar as if they owned it. Coming out of the sunshine, it took a moment for their eyes to become used to the gloom. The room had about thirty people sitting or standing and chatting among themselves. The newcomers seemed to be looking for someone, their eyes scanned the bar and landed on Maria. They strode purposefully over to the table, Brody could tell this was not going to end well. He smiled and looked up at these two rough goons, obviously looking for booze and trouble.

Brody was brought back to the moment as he was suddenly hit in the side of the head with a straight right from out of the blue. The big Russian's friend had taken advantage of the situation by flanking him, stepping out from behind a fridge, and throwing an easy punch. The arm behind it was strong from years of hard work. Brody slammed against the wall, cursing himself for losing his concentration. Walloping the wall with the flat of his back, he knew he had to act fast or this would get serious in a hurry. The second Russian came for him again, figuring after the clout to the head he could get in easily and break his opponent. This guy was as big as his drinking companion, sweating from the high temperature and the physical exertion. The newcomer to the fight was about 6' 4", in his late forties or early fifties. Like his friend, he had once been very fit. Maybe from the Russian armed forces, but nothing special, probably just a grunt. He had huge hands, ones you did not want to be hit with, knuckles that were red and broken from many bar fights over the years, and a flaming scar across his right cheek. If they had come off a ship, then this was their R and R, and they were going to have some fun, like it or not. The first guy was taking a break, having a drink at the bar, panting with exertion, smiling towards Brody as he got his breath back before coming in for the kill. The rest of the crowd in the room were just watching the floor show. Brody felt like a dancing bear on a chain brought in for the amusement of the crowd.

He went into tactical drill mode as his training took over. Honed reflexes kicked in, no thinking, just fast, decisive action.

The hours and hours of drill, the years of practice and the missions he had been on in the Special Boat Service all came together in a split second. His muscles had so much memory they had forgotten more than these two brutes had ever known. Brody watched as the first guy came in to finish him off. He was in a tight corner with blocks either side, it looked bad, but he had trained in close and very close quarter combat. Fighting in a small space had been literally beaten into him. His Sargent Major's voice came into his head: "Son, when you're in a corner, fight like a rat, anything goes, eyes, ears, nose, throat and balls. Get the lot as quick and hard as you can."

The guy couldn't get his swing in as he was in close to the wall. He decided to try some boxing jabs. Brody, now fully awake, parried them one at a time, looking for an opportunity. The big guy was trying to concentrate on his opponent's face but could not touch him as Brody was moving or blocking the slow blows with ease. The giant Russian dropped his guard for a second. Brody took his chance and struck, a straight punch from the shoulder, just a jab really, but designed to stop. The Russian did just that, he could not believe his nose had just been broken again. The blood came gushing, and his eyes started to water. This just enraged him further, his opponent was supposed to crumble at the first blow. This was not so much fun, hitting back was not meant to be part of the deal.

The Russian decided it was time to end the charade and go for the kill. He threw a killer punch straight at Brody's face, aiming to inflict the same amount of damage as had been done to him seconds before. The problem with his strategy was, it was the exact thing that was expected. Brody was standing there, waiting for him to come up with the idea. The punch registered on the Russian's face long before the thought moved from his brain down through his arm and finally into his fist. Brody watched in very slow motion as the fist clenched and wound up for the hard-straight jab directly at his nose, aiming to shatter the small bones. Then push them into his face, causing severe long-term damage that would be hard to fix here in Africa. It finally came barreling forward, full of power. This guy was still strong, but not so fast anymore, he was like an old boxer way past his prime trying to keep up with the young bucks on the scene. Brody simply slid down the wall, bending his knees. The fist hit the cinder block wall, causing more pain, shattering the bones of the fingers and knuckles. Then Brody gave a nasty uppercut into the Russians balls in one swift movement, ducking out to the left as the guy fell to the floor groaning, bleeding and probably with some broken fingers.

When the two goons had approached their table earlier and confronted them, they seemed to know Maria. She shyly feigned innocence, saying she did not want to speak to them. This had gotten Brody's gentlemanly side up, there was no other option than to protect the poor girl's honor, a real knight in shining armor. Of course, this must be a case of mistaken identity, she was a tourist, for God's sake, on holiday. When the guys had started to argue, apparently, the big fat one had taken her home the night before, and they had agreed to meet today to continue the festivities. Brody did not believe them for a minute and told the guys to bug off and leave them to their afternoon.

That was when it had gotten out of hand. The big fat Russian had pushed Brody away from the table almost knocking his chair over. Brody had not taken this well, jumping to his feet he pushed them back with a very hard shove knocking some tables over and spilling drinks on the dirt floor.

Brody had been drinking for about four hours. First, the local lager, 'Tusker', which was what everyone drank, then some really cheap whiskey chasers. Belligerence was the order of the day.

That had been it, an already very tricky situation had moved to a very dangerous one very quickly. The next thing Brody knew, he was flying through the air and rolling over a table.

The last guy looked at his friend on the floor in an ever-increasing pool of blood, one hand clasped over his nose and the other between his legs. This was not meant to happen, not in Africa. It was always so easy here. The locals just let them do what they wanted, and the tourists were scared of their own shadow. He emitted a guttural roar of rage, like a mother lion after her precious cub has just been dragged off into the bush by a pack of hyenas. Then he came charging through the room towards Brody at full speed, there was no stopping him. Brody dodged to the left slightly. The Russian kept coming, putting his head down to take Brody's legs away with his shoulders. The thug's plan was simple: pick him up and slam him against the wall instantly crushing his body, maybe even breaking his back with the impact. Brody watched the charge carefully. He had to time this right, or he could end up dead. The huge Russian kept running, adjusting to get his full weight behind the charge, oblivious to everything else. This guy was past angry, the red curtain had fallen across his vision it was death or die trying. Brody stepped a little more to his left, watching the guy adjust. He was so angry all he could see was his target. When impact was imminent, Brody could smell the sweat and anger pulsating off his attacker. His assailant was full of Russian rage, out to kill. All sense had left him. Brody pushed off the giant's shoulders, landing neatly on the balls of his feet, four feet to the left.

The whole building shook, a tremor rattled the glasses on the bar. Several large fruit bats flew from the Makuti roof, where they had been sleeping the day off, frightened by the sudden vibration. Brody had positioned himself in front of the large upright tree trunk holding the ceiling in place. The Russian's head connected with it full force. The crack sounded very final, like a butcher's cleaver chopping a joint of meat. The post was entirely unharmed, not a scratch, but the same could not be said for the human being that had collided with it. The trunk was probably more than one hundred years old and hard as iron. The head that hit it was soft, almost an eggshell, the battle was totally one-sided.

The Russian fell flat on his face in the dirt. Blood was coming from the top of his head. He groaned and lay still. Brody hoped he was only out cold! You could hear a pin drop in the bar.

Maria grabbed Brody's hand and said. "Let's move, we can't stay here now!" In a second they were out on what amounted to a curb. It was not broad enough to be called a pavement. In their rush to escape, they almost fell into a deep drainage ditch, filled with stagnant water and rubbish, running beside the road.

This town was the go-to place for every semi-truck heading north. The massive fourteen and sixteen wheelers thundered across the twisted bridge over the creek heading into the melee, on a one-lane, pothole-filled road.

The trucks, mostly with two forty-foot containers on the back, full way beyond capacity, raced into town, belching diesel smoke, grinding gears with horns blasting and air brakes hissing. This combined with the hundreds of small motorbikes, 'PikiPiki's,' manically maneuvering up and down the road between the trucks and people. The air was filled with the smell of roasting meat, every meat conceivable from donkey right through to camel, smoke and diesel fumes.

Crossing the road, they dodged a huge truck racing into town and blasting its horn angrily, then raced into the markets of Mtwappa. Maria seemed to know her way around this place too well for a tourist from Nairobi. But Brody was just following, trying to get his wits about him. The market had blaring music, T-shirts, gold watches, pots and pans, TVs and radios. More cooking meat, Coke stands, a man selling sausages from a cart, another selling mangoes with a lady shouting something Brody could not understand. It was sensory overload, like a nightmare, full of noise and movement.

Everything was happening all at once around him. Faces laughing and smiling, holding stuff out to him as he flashed by. A guy grabbed his shirt to try to show him something. Brody spun, pushing him away back into his stall, ignoring the shouts and insults from the disgruntled owner. They were weaving through the center of this cacophony of sound and motion, darting this way and that. Brody jumped over a large fat lady sat in the middle of the path. She had a huge cauldron of scalding hot cooking oil over a charcoal fire with lumps of potato bubbling on the surface, shouting "Viazi A Kari" at the top of her lungs.

They came out of one set of stalls into a small rubbish-strewn lane with dismantled motorcycle parts all over the floor. A couple of young lads were squat on the floor in the dust with some old spanners, repairing the vehicles. Brody almost collided with the massive furry chest of a camel. The beast hissed, lashing out with its hoof then spitting at him. The young Somali on the back of the camel started shouting insults from above. They raced on.

Maria was dragging Brody along through the crowd. Twisting and turning in and out of the people and market stalls. He had a problem keeping up. She grabbed his hand, shouting, "We must hurry, we don't want the cops arresting us. That would be trouble, you don't want to go inside!"

She pulled him down narrow alleys, smelling like open sewers, then across small busy roads where everyone was doing something and shouting about it. You could buy anything here from a Kalashnikov to a new Toyota, probably not exactly new, perhaps still warm from the last owner.

Finally, Maria ducked between some washing lines across someone's back yard, into the main street again and immediately entered a ladies' hair salon, she shouted. "Hi, Mum!" Before Brody could ask any questions, she dragged him out the back-door and into an adjoining bar, where she calmly walking up to the bartender and said, "Hi Chiro. Two cold Tuskers."

Brody was shocked. He had just been through a wash cycle and spin. His head was taking a moment to catch up. The race through the village had started in an easterly direction for about 200 yards. Then a sharp turn to the northeast, running through the market stalls, this had gone on for six hundred running strides about a mile. Another turn west for about three hundred yards. This put his current location, about one and a half miles north-west of the bar. *Shukran* would be to his south-east about two miles away at her mooring. He had learned a lot as they had run and would return to assess the new routes through the village and have a look at some of the shops along the way, everything was committed to memory.

He stared at Maria, but she just smiled that beautiful smile, "Man, you can fight. That was so cool, I've never seen anything like that before."

Brody slumped in a chair, accepting his cold Tusker gratefully. He took a long pull on the ice-cold liquid, slowly letting it glide down his dry and parched throat. After a couple of minutes, he was getting his senses back. He went over the afternoon's events, and took particular note that his new tourist friend had shouted 'Hi, Mum' as she had run through the salon next door. It was as clear as the smile on her face, Maria was not quite what she had said she was.

Brody wandered over to the bar where Maria was sat. It was easy to see why men could get caught by this beautiful young girl. There were so many thoughts running through his head. He should confront this obvious con woman, after defending her honor like a bloody idiot! Then, like pulling a rabbit out of a hat, she slapped an old brown wallet on the counter, opened it, and handed a 1000-shilling note to the bartender. That was enough for ten beers. Brody looked at it in astonishment.

He reached out and snatched the wallet from Maria. "Hey!" She shouted, "That's mine!"

Brody sneered, "Yeah right. You look like Markov Slidivoga. You stole it off those Russian guys."

Maria replied, "Ah a girl's gotta eat, you know. This ain't cheap," as she slapped her own behind.

"Anyway, it was hanging out of his pocket. If I hadn't done it then somebody else would have. It's man eat man out there," she replied.

Brody looked at her, "You are some piece of work you know."

She answered with her big brown eyes as large as saucers, "AND! Your point is?"

Brody said, "You have to give this back. If he doesn't have his ID, he won't be able to get back on his ship, or he might end up in jail."

"Man, you are a good guy. Those big Russians were about to tear you apart."

Brody replied, "That's different."

He thought it was probably all Maria's fault anyway, they were just innocent marks!

Maria looked at him and shrugged, "OK no problem, I will let them have their wallet back, but the cash is mine." Brody was in no position to argue this point. As far as he was concerned, he was in enemy territory with an opponent who had far greater knowledge of the local surroundings.

Maria ordered two more Tuskers. For a girl she could drink, another endearing point thought

Brody. When the drinks had arrived, she shouted, "Sunshine! Sunshine!" A few minutes later, a young lad of about 12 years of age came shyly out from the backroom or kitchen as it seemed to be, there were bangs and clattering from that general direction. The boy came over to Maria. She frowned at him, he turned to Brody, held out his hand, and said. "Good afternoon, sir, how are you today?"

Brody grinned, "I am fine sir thank you."

Formalities over, Maria reached into her bag and took out 100 shillings, about a dollar, then said, "Sunshine Mwangi, I want you to go straight to the Police Base, you find Corporal Naivasha and hand this over to him. Say someone left it on the road and you picked it up, it was empty when you found it, OK?" Sunshine nodded eagerly, his eyes fixed on the crisp new note. He grabbed the money and the wallet, then raced out through the door to the hair salon. The bar was immediately filled with the smell of perfume and hairspray, and the sound of ladies laughing and shouting as the door slammed behind the young boy.

Maria said, "That's my mom's salon. She does the beauty, and my dad does the beer!"

She went on, "We are Kikuyu. My father lost his job on the tea plantation about ten years ago. We had nothing. Then my aunt who had come to Mtwappa to find a 'Muzungu,' (a white or European guy), called him and told him Mtwappa was a good place to make money. My mom was from the village. She could not speak any English, only Kikuyu. When we arrived, she was lost, just wandering around the town looking for things to do. We Kikuyu are hardworking people. As she was walking and looking around, she heard the 'whites' saying 'isn't it a beautiful day, such a lot of sunshine,' Then she heard someone say, 'Hello, Sunshine.' She fell in love with the word. About eight months after when her son was born, she demanded he be called 'Sunshine Mwangi.' My dad was furious. He should have been called Mwangi Sunshine!" Maria laughed at her own joke.

As they were chatting, a plate of meat had arrived with chapatti, a flatbread made from flour and water, cooked on a flat pan over the fire. The simple meal was served with a mixture of onions, chili, and tomatoes. Maria explained that it was Kachumbari, their local salad. Brody surveyed the meat suspiciously, Maria laughed, and said. "Don't worry, that's chicken. You can see the bones." She picked a leg, hungrily setting about the barbequed meat.

"If you want the camel, ask for the beef and if you want donkey, ask for the Samosas." She said through mouthfuls. These were small triangular shaped pies, deep-fried and filled with a variety of different ingredients, from vegetables through to any non-descript meat that might be hanging around.

Brody sat back and took a long pull on his beer. This had been a strange day, he thought. It started out well, a bit rough in the middle, but then getting better at the end. Maria was a tough street kid. Brody felt for her, he knew a bit about living on the streets. He had been brought up in Central London in a place called Wood Green on the council estates. spending most of his time away from school, wandering down to the city and gazing at the river, dreaming of sailing off into the sunset, or heading off on his bike packed high with gear to find a place to set up camp in the woods and forests outside of London. The council estates had not been easy and school worse. He had not done well, leaving at sixteen then immediately joining the Marines.

Maria was cute and good company though Brody knew he had to keep an eye on his wallet and her hands. But they seemed to have crossed a point: they were friends now, he was no longer her next mark. Or so he hoped. The afternoon wore on, the beer kept coming, and the food and company were good. Brody met Maria's father, Mr Mwangi, he was in his sixties, small and wiry with a dark brown, knowing face, a wrinkled brow, and long arms that had seen work. He grinned at Brody, then Maria interjected in Kikuyu. Brody did not understand. When Maria had finished, she turned to Brody and said, "I told him you saved me and my honor, and you are not to be conned for anything. Not even the beer. I told him to charge you regular price and not steal your wallet."

Brody laughed out loud. This place was a madhouse.

After Mr Mwangi had agreed not to con Brody, they became instant friends. He ran the bar plus other pursuits he did not want to go into in front of Wanjiku or Maria. He kept correcting himself, Maria's Kikuyu name was Wanjiku. Brody instantly liked the name and started using it at once.

They ate and drank the afternoon away on the Russian's money. It was dark when Brody thought he should head home. Wanjiku walked him to the crowded street. She then entered into a lengthy and rapid negotiation with a motorcycle taxi, small, 100 hp Chinese models of famous bikes. The drivers earnt their cash by giving people rides around the town. This form of transport was precarious, to say the least. The drivers would often have just started riding a bike in the morning and were ready as taxi men by lunchtime. A helmet was out of the question and just laughed off. Wanjiku said it would only ruin her hair anyway so she never wore one! Brody was instructed to only give 100 shillings when he got to the mooring of *Shukran*. He headed off into the night, making plans to see Wanjiku again, he was beginning to like this place.

Chapter Two

The smell of strong Arabic coffee was in the air. The burning charcoal of the small coal burner used to heat the water to make the coffee in the way only the Arabs know. The early morning sounds of an old wooden dhow waking up were beginning. The gentle slapping of the small waves against the side of the wooden boat. Timbers gently creaked against one another. The weaver bird's incessant twittering, in the trees, overhanging the lazy creek. These small brightly-coloured birds fussed and squawked at their mates, fighting for space on the branches, getting ready to repair their nests, and find food for their young. Brody slowly came back to life. It was about another twenty or thirty minutes until the sun would start to show its glowing head and slowly burn its way up from the horizon. The darkness was gone, just a gloom patiently waiting for the new day to arrive. The haunting wail of the cleric calling his faithful to prayer wafted through the early morning mist covering the creek.

    Fishermen were already starting their day's work, paddling out to the mouth of the creek about one mile further east where the freshwater mingled with the salt and it all became the Indian Ocean. They would not return until late in the afternoon, hopefully with enough fish to feed their families. If they were lucky, there might even be a few left to sell.

Brody came back to consciousness with the memories of the day before still lingering in his mind. Wanjiku was stuck there, her wonderful smile and conman ways made him grin as he gradually came back to the land of the living.

Hassan, his First Mate and good friend, approached with a tiny cup and a conical shaped copper coffee pot on a large ornate tray. He had been buying unusual items when they were in Mombasa a few miles south of Mtwappa. The coffee pot and tray were now prized possessions. The coffee pot was about 12 inches tall with a flat circular bottom then coming to a point at the top, about two-thirds of the way up the lid was just a seam. The pot had an ornate handle and was used specifically for this excellent aromatic Arabian coffee Hassan seemed to be able to create from nowhere.

Gratefully taking the small cup being offered, he started waking up. Hassan asked, "Mr Brody we need to do some work on *Shukran*, can we do it here on the beach? The sand is white, there is no mud, it will be easy."

Brody replied, "How are the tides?"

Hassan took a second to look at the sky, then said, "The water will be high today around noon,

Bwana. We can take her out and put her on the beach, then do the Kalifati."

Brody just nodded in agreement. He was learning fast about maintenance on a wooden boat, but still knew that Hassan was in charge in this area.

Hassan went off to start his day and get his shipmate Gumbao ready for the day's activities.

Brody's daily routine of running about five to six miles was incredibly important. Going without a good run for a few days left him feeling like a man waking from a coma, slow, with a thick head, not sure what was happening around him. There were other benefits too. It cleared his head allowing the thoughts to flow smoothly after pumping some good endorphins into his body. Running in the early mornings had been part of his life for as long as he could remember. After joining the Marines, the training instructors had punished the new recruits with running long arduous treks into the wilderness of the UK's moorlands and mountains: looking to weed out the weakest of the group, so only the fit survived. Brody had loved the competition, pushing his body further each day, willing the instructors to ask for more. Then the Special Boat Service (S.B.S) was a whole new ball game. Just to get through the interviews you had to be the strongest of the strong. The S.B.S torturers, as they liked to be known, enjoyed the first few weeks of training. Every new recruit was like a lamb to the slaughter, the torturers called it beasting which meant pushing the recruit to the absolute limits of exhaustion. And then beyond. It was like a Japanese Prisoner of War Camp combined with the Spanish Inquisition, the beastings were to make you fail, that was the object of the game. Trudging through the snow, like a pack mule climbing an ice-covered mountain in a blizzard in temperatures of minus four degrees, you just got beaten until you dropped or survived. Most failed, but to Brody, it was like heroin to an addict. He hated to love it and always wanted more.

Brody ran along beside the creek, heading out towards the ocean. The beach was almost empty apart from a few fishermen pushing their solid, heavy dugout canoes into the water for the day's work, hunting the elusive fish in the mangrove swamps. After running for so many years, his body and brain had an integral milometer fixed in place. Running, and distance gauging, was automatic. His muscles knew when he had reached the three miles and it was time to turn back. The return route was always harder, pushing him that little bit more each day. Running along the edge of the mangroves, leaping across the twisted branches, then finding the softest sand and powering through it until his thighs screamed at him to stop, but he would just push on back to *Shukran*. Arriving at the boat, he would immediately dive off the side into the warm waters of the creek. Swimming to the halfway point, about one hundred yards off the beach, and returning with a final blast of energy. A hard-free stroke, like an Olympic swimmer heading for the gold.

Hassan had been traveling with Brody for the best part of a year now. He was an unassuming, very friendly guy, about 5' 4" tall with a thin, wiry frame, very quick smile and always laughing, dark brown, sharp eyes and strong callused fisherman hands. He usually wore a white or multi-colored turban, a T-shirt, and shorts then a small Kanzu over the top. The Kanzu was like a long gown the Swahilis wear, usually white or brown in color, with embroidery around the collar and cuffs. Hassan had been a sailor since he was a small boy, leaving school before his twelfth birthday then seeing a business opportunity, he had taught himself English, enabling him to work with the tourists that regularly came on the weekly ferry to his home on Pemba Island. These short-term visitors always paid well. They did not seem to know how cheap life in Africa was, or they felt guilty for being so rich, Hassan did not know or care really. During the offseason, he would fish with his dad out in the Pemba Channel, the forty-mile-wide passage between Pemba and the mainland of Tanzania. Now things were different. He had been lucky, Allah had smiled down on him. The regular monthly income from Mr Brody was enough for his family to live and his sister to go to school. She was the clever one.

Hassan had met Mr Brody on Pemba Island, a real stroke of good fortune. After watching the new

'Muzungu' jump off the ferry onto the rickety wooden jetty and get his pile of stuff passed down to him, Hassan had moved in with his usual casual smile and offer of help. After a few minutes of chatting about what the new visitor was looking for and what he wanted, it was evident to Hassan that this one was a bit different. His eyes were cold and dark, always darting this way and that as if expecting an attack at any second. There was no smile at all, which is very strange to an African. Smiling is a way of life. His new friend seemed to be like a caged animal that had suddenly been let loose to run free. Unsure what to do or how to do it, having never been free, the existence was alien to him. Swahilis are very friendly and open, especially on the Islands. This guy was the complete opposite, closed and dangerous. After offering his small wooden dhow and promising peace and quiet with no fuss, the cold dark stranger opened up slightly, explaining he was here to dive in the quiet calm reefs and lagoons Pemba had to offer. He would stay for as long as he wanted, he had nowhere else to go.

After some fun with negotiations, they had settled on a daily figure for the use of the small boat with Hassan as the captain. The next was accommodation. Hassan knew the routine and played along as always, acting the idiot until he could get the tourist to trust him, then sending them to his uncle's guest house, passing by later for a hefty commission. But this guy was different. Hassan soon sensed if he tried any of the usual tricks he would get in trouble very quickly. His new customer felt dangerous enough without being angry. Instead, he had opted for the small chalet on the beach his family-owned. It was more of a fishing shack really with none of the amenities the 'Muzungus' always had to have. Hassan knew it would be perfect for his friend as it was quiet, out of the way with no fuss. He had been right; the guy took it immediately without another word.

That had been a long time ago. They had now become firm friends, traveling the length of Kenya, rescuing Hassan's sister, and foiling a plot by some radical jihadists. This was how Mr Brody had become the proud owner of the dhow known as *Shukran*. Hassan's grandfather had been so happy to have his only granddaughter returned to the family safe and sound that he had decided immediately to make a gift of an old dhow he had owned for many years to their savior. In the end, the whole village had contributed, repairing the engine, and making the boat seaworthy. Once everything was ready, Hassan had been dispatched to invite Mr Brody back for a celebration where the old wooden boat was presented to him. That plus a small pouch of uncut diamonds from an East Indiaman hold wrecked off Pemba 100 years before. During some diving off the west coast of Pemba, they had found an old sword from India, this had led them to a lost treasure hidden in caves on the coast. Hassan could see his new friend was beginning to change, with occasional smiles the dark, haunted eyes had left. Mr Brody was laughing and enjoying life. All he had to do now was find him a good Swahili woman then he would be set!

Hassan had taken Mr Brody to the markets of Mombasa on the way up from Pemba. The distance from Pemba to Mombasa is about sixty-five nautical miles sailing roughly north, north-east along the coast. Once they had arrived in Mombasa old town, Hassan, and their other shipmate Gumbao, had taken over the whole situation. After docking at the small local jetty leading into the dark, narrow streets of Old Town, Gumbao had led them to an old friend of his, Dalali or Lali for short. Lali was the kind of guy who knows everyone and sells everything, the local wheeler-dealer. Soon they were sat at the back of a jewelry store called Fat Buddha, drinking tea and negotiating over the diamonds. Hassan was sure the deal had not been in their favor. But when the Indian started piling more money than he had ever seen before on the floor for them to count, he had not argued. And the best part was they had only sold a quarter of their stash, they could live like kings forever on this!

Gumbao was another new friend of Mr Brody's, he did not say much though. He was a bit older than Mr Brody in his late forties, and a little shorter than his almost six feet, with closely cropped white hair, a furrowed brow from constantly frowning into the sun while at sea, long loose limbs with hands that were curled from dragging fishing nets on board his whole life. His palms and fingers were hard and dry as sandpaper, the nails all cracked or gone from hard work. When Hassan looked at him, he saw a guy with no worries at all. Each new day was a good one, as it had arrived and he was part of it. He never had any money in his pockets, just an excellent attitude which seemed to get him where he needed to be. He was not a Muslim, which upset Hassan a little. Gumbao was a Giriama, a coastal tribe that still believed in witchcraft.

Gumbao's feet had never seen shoes in his life, easily a size twelve or thirteen and flat as pancakes with soles like animal hide. On a sunbaked deck, he could walk with no feeling when Mr Brody was hopping from foot to foot. Gumbao was a big tough fisherman with a taste for the drink. He could find it when no other could, disappearing into thin air then sometimes reappearing hours or days later, either drunk already or carrying some sort of booze. Gumbao was always ready to help, great in a fight, with an easy, toothless smile.

The head man on Pemba had asked Mr Brody to take the then sleeping Gumbao away with them when they left. He had been drinking the local brew made from fermenting coconut milk. When exposed to the sun, it immediately starts rotting and smells like cream left outside on a hot summers day. This stench permeates from the drinker's skin. Gumbao slept on the deck, no one would go near him for a good two days. On the third day, after slowly coming around, he demanded cigarettes, booze, and finally some water. All he had were the clothes on his back which amounted to a T-shirt and a pair of shorts. The new situation he found himself in did not seem to faze him. After taking a day to fully recover, he tied a rope around his waist and jumped over the side of the dhow to be dragged along for a good mile. When his cleansing session was over, he decided in usual African fashion that as he was older than Hassan, his rightful place was second in command. Then life continued, no complaints, just another day on the ocean fishing and sailing. This was the African way. You could uproot someone then just pretty much press-gang them onto a boat then get no complaints at all. Hassan smiled as he thought of the tourists that visited Pemba Island. How they needed sun cream, bottled water, special shoes for the beach, and shirts to ward off the sun.

The sun was slowly burning the dew off the decks of *Shukran*. Hassan was busy today. There was work to do, with leaks below the waterline the crew had to get her out of the water to apply the 'Kalifati.' Gumbao was essential to the job, although since he had taken on the role of second in command, Hassan had decided to ignore him and carry on as usual. They had to push *Shukran* up the beach during the high tide around saa nane, two o'clock in the afternoon. Then he remembered the stupid 'Muzungus' did not understand proper time so he adjusted in his head to two o'clock or as Bwana Brody said, 14:00, like a soldier. The 'Muzungu' time really was confusing; his Swahili time was much better and easier. When the sun came up properly, it was the first hour of the day, Saa Moja, Hour One, this was for 'Muzungus' 7 am. Then you went along second-hour third hour and so on until you reached the 12, by then it would be dark which was around 6 pm 'Muzungu' time. You started again for the night time at one, which was 7 pm and went around again until 12 which would be the hour just before sunrise. So easy and yet the 'Muzungus' always had to complicate stuff!

Hassan was enjoying his new job as First Mate on *Shukran*. it meant he got to practice his English with Mr Brody and sail all over the place. Mr Brody had left his mom and dad with six months' salary as they would not be returning for a while. The radicals, or the Kaya Bombo, as they were known, had tried to kill them. So, the head elder had sent Mr Brody and Hassan away until things cooled off.

But today they had to get *Shukran* up on the beach. Hassan was looking everywhere for Gumbao. He had gone missing the night before after dinner and had not been seen since. The morning was starting. It was almost 06:00, they had to get everything ready before the tide started leaving again at 14:00. There was a lot to do. *Shukran* was a wooden boat and needed extra care. She could not just be dragged up the beach and left.

Hassan had spoken to some of his cousins who had agreed to arrive at around 08:00 to help, bringing with them some stout wooden poles about nine feet long. These poles would be buried in the sand up to about a foot, then leaned against *Shukran* from either side to hold her upright until the water came again to support her.

This was a precarious job. If the pole either sank into the sand or slipped out, *Shukran* would fall onto her side. This was very dangerous as the rising tide would flood her before they could float her again, ruining the engine and splitting planks. Hassan was anxious that this did not happen, so he performed his duties as the First Mate very seriously.

Gumbao turned up an hour later, looking very pleased with himself.

Hassan snapped sarcastically, "Where have you been, Boss?"

Gumbao said, "Ah you see, I was walking along the road, up where the big trucks are, looking for a friend of mine who owes me money. Then I heard a sound like click, click and shouting, so I had to go see what was happening. You would never believe it, but there was a certain group playing checkers in a small bar off the main road. Now you know I like a game. I'm no gambler but if someone wants to give me their money, who am I to say no. These guys were locals, not a professional like me. I sat patiently, then when it was my turn to play, I took them for everything. LOOK, I won this shirt, then these pants, I even took this hat off a stupid tourist who was watching us."

He had a brand-new ocean blue Hawaiian shirt with green parrots and hula girls dancing around his waist, a pair of extra-long orange shorts, with a bright purple baseball cap, proudly proclaiming, in bold black letters, he was a 'TOURIST.'

Hassan looked at his crewmate in amazement. "We have work to do. You can't be messing around like this, I told you last night to get here on time."

Gumbao joked, "Ah you are just a boy, you don't understand. All will be OK, the water is only just coming, I had everything planned in my head."

Hassan was lost for words. It was like fighting the wind, a total waste of your life. He just shook his head and carried on with his day's work.

They prepared *Shukran* by stowing all the gear they could safely out of the way and under the decks. Then they walked the beach, looking for debris or rocks which might foul her, or worse still put pressure on the keel. The next job was to make a marker point on the beach to head for when the boat was being driven onto shore. As they were finishing, Hassan's cousins arrived. They were all business. It was past noon and they had to get a move on. Inching *Shukran* off the jetty where she was moored, Brody drove carefully with Hassan giving instructions. Reaching the center of the channel, Brody came about one hundred and eighty degrees, then started motoring down the creek towards the ocean. They knew they had to catch the slack tide when the water was not coming or going.

Brody did a few circles, then Hassan ordered him to head straight for the shore at dead slow. He had to keep feathering the engines, making sure *Shukran* held a straight and steady course towards the marker. Gumbao was up to his chest in the water, giving more directions, left and right to Hassan, which were then conveyed to Brody. Finally, there were eight more guys in the water, up to their waists, holding the posts ready and waiting.

Edging closer to the beach until the boat was about thirty feet away, Hassan signaled Brody, to cut the engine with a slicing of his throat. Hassan threw a line to Gumbao as *Shukran* slowly drifted in towards the beach on the last of the momentum from the propeller. Once Gumbao could grab the bow, he hauled *Shukran* in as far as he dared, leaving only about four inches under the keel.

Then the boys started moving around the outside of *Shukran*, placing the poles in the sand until they were firm, then leaning them in until they stuck under the rubbing strip. This would support *Shukran* while the 'Kalifati' was being completed.

Once *Shukran* had the eight poles supporting her, the boys took the anchor far up the beach, setting it firmly in the sand. Lines were taken from the stern, port, and starboard sides to several trees to ensure she held her position as she settled onto the sand.

When Hassan was satisfied she was set, he left Gumbao sitting on the beach watching *Shukran* and headed off for the 'Kalifati Fundi.' Brody had been on hand the whole time, helping with the poles and setting *Shukran* straight. He was now unemployed until the water receded, so he decided to head over to the local bar the 'Full Moon'. The place was idyllic, right on the creek with views all the way to the ocean. It was built on reclaimed land with a sturdy sea wall which Brody had used to moor *Shukran*. The water was lapping high on the wall, but Brody knew it was already heading back out to the ocean. He sat at a small wooden table and ordered his Tusker, making sure it was a cold one. Wanjiku had taught him the word 'Baridi,' meaning cold in Swahili, a very useful term. Relaxing in the afternoon sun, idly watching the pied kingfishers dart above the water, then dive-bomb straight into the creek and come up with a small soldierfish or a baby skipjack. The place was full of life if you sat and watched for a while and let the world go by. Brody could see several silver gray barracuda swimming below him lazily, moving in the current, waiting for night to fall when they would head out again to hunt. Life was good. His mind wandered to the firefights in Somalia and the trudges through the jungle in The Congo, or Zaire as it was called then. He had earned a break after the many years of training or fighting, almost twenty when he had finally decided to get out. That was a long time to be holding a gun, crisscrossing the world so many times he could not remember. Always landing in some out of the way place, or coming into a beach he had never seen and never would again. Then creeping around for days, weeks or even months looking for an elusive enemy.

Sitting quietly deep in thought, a polite cough startled him. A large white guy was standing with the sun behind his back, holding a glass of dark liquid in one hand and a beer in the other.

He smiled, "Gooday, mate, me name's Barry. I'm the manager of this place, and general dog's body. Do you mind if I take a load off? I brought you a cold one on the house."

Brody offered a chair, Barry gratefully sat, "Cheers mate."

Handing Brody the beer, he took a large swallow of the whiskey in his glass, then held it up in the air shouting, "Bring me another!" A waiter casually ambled over and took the glass for a refill. This was obviously not the first time this had happened.

Barry was a big chap in every way, about 6'6" tall and about that around the waist too, with a dark mop of thinning hair, and at least two days' growth of dark whiskers on his chin. He had cobalt blue, clear eyes that were quick to shine when he smiled, which was often, and a faraway gaze like all sailors, checking the weather and the swells. The large wooden chair groaned as he sat and looked at the creek in front of him. A long moment passed as they both gazed at the incredible scenery. Barry said, "Bloody paradise mate, isn't it. Eh."

Brody replied, "You are not wrong there, I could get used to this."

Then Barry's drink arrived.

Barry had stopped here on a round-the-world sailing trip about eight years ago and never left. His beautiful sixty-five-foot catamaran was moored in the creek.

He explained, "Well, mate, I was on the way up the coast. I was going to go through the Suez and head into the Med, but this place just grabbed me. The owner here was getting on a bit and let me come in as manager come everything, meaning, I pretty much have a free hand to run the place. I can tell you it has suited me, I live on me boat and work here."

Brody thought for a minute. It is fantastic how people make their lives: one minute they are sailing the world, the next they're a bar manager on the East African Coast.

They chatted a while about the creek and *Shukran*. Brody enjoyed the conversation. Barry was full of information about Mtwappa and the surrounding area.

Brody asked, "Barry, do you know any good diving in the area."

Barry said, "Well mate I am not much of a diver, as you can see," he said, pointing at his stomach, "But I know a man who does. I'll find him and get him to come around tomorrow." This was great news. While *Shukran* was being repaired, Brody could get in a few dives.

Hassan had brought the Fundi back to the beach several hours ago, first helping to set up the expert's tools then showing him the leaks in the planks. Once the Fundi had settled on a mat on the soft sand under *Shukran's* belly, he prepared his small hammer, the oil, and the 'Kalifati', which was waste cotton that came in large bundles. Hassan had bought it in Old Town Mombasa along with the simsim oil, the Swahili word for sesame. The old man started rolling lines of the waste cotton out between his palms like long thin sausages, then carefully poured the oil into his cupped hands, rolling the cotton between them briskly. Once he was satisfied the oil had penetrated the waste cotton, he laid the long roll of what was now 'Kalifati' into the lines between the planks, then tapped it in with the small hammer and chisel. There was now a flexible, waterproof seal between the two planks. As the boat moved in the ocean, the 'Kalifati' would slowly get worn away. The fish also loved to eat the cotton to get at the oil.

This was a long slow process. Hassan watched intently. He had seen it done a hundred times before, but now wanted it to be perfect for his *Shukran*. Swahilis are a very social tribe of East Africa. Any meeting of two people turns into a lengthy debate, chatting about everything under the sun. The old Fundi and Hassan put the world to rights as they did their work. The Fundi spotted a loose plank, then found a couple of rusted nails which he pulled out. After more discussion, the hardwood plank was cleaned up and recut to fit. Some Kalifati was placed in any open spaces as the wood was tapped back into place. More of the soaked cotton waste was wrapped around a large flat head of a new shiny nail and hammered home.

Brody could hear the *tap-tap* from the boat as they drank in the bar. Barry asked, "Mate. These wooden boats, they have a weird sail. How do you manage them?"

Brody replied, "They're called Lateen sails. They have been used along this coast for hundreds of years, back when they traded slaves."

Barry pointed across the creek to a beautiful Catamaran sat at a mooring. She was long and sleek, a real ocean-going sailing craft. He said, "So I sailed from New Zealand through to Indonesia, then across to Thailand, and to India, and Goa, across the Indian Ocean to here. It was a journey I can tell you. But the Cat is a good boat. Nearly fifty feet long, she can go through anything mother nature has to offer. My sails are all run on electric winches, mate. It's a piece of piss really, sailing like that, just pressing buttons.

Brody smiled. "This is entirely different. We have to haul the boom up to the top of the mast with pulleys and lines, then set the sail. Tacking and jibing is a bugger especially when the sail is wet."

"It looks like bloody hard work to me. I think I'll stick to my own. She's a beaut, though, can't deny you that," Barry said looking at *Shukran*.

Brody just smiled and took a sip of his beer

Barry asked, "So mate, where do you store the guns?"

Brody looked at him in astonishment, "What guns?"

Barry looked back with equal astonishment, "You got to have some protection here, mate. You never know what might happen. And out there." Barry pointed to the ocean, "That's the bloody Wild West, mate!"

Brody said, "No guns on *Shukran*. I wouldn't know where to get them anyway."

Barry looked at Brody and broke into a smile, "Good, mate. I might just be able to help you there if you're interested?"

Brody was interested. He knew that being armed was a good thing, especially when sailing around this coastline. There were stories of pirates operating in these waters, ruthless cutthroats that would kill the crew without a thought, then take off with the boat, selling it or using it to smuggle their contraband. A bit of firepower would give him serious peace of mind.

Brody said, "Why not? I can see your point. What you offering?"

"Ah, not me mate, we have to go and see a guy."

Brody replied, "Cool, whenever you're free."

Barry was on his feet in a second, "No time like the present, mate."

They finished up their drinks and headed off to the car park at the back of the Full Moon. Barry had a big, old, white, four-door, 109" long wheelbase Landrover. Brody knew these cars, he had used them in the desert.

Barry said, "Brody, meet the Loner. She's a beaut, but she is a real bitch. Reminds me of my second wife. She wouldn't wake up in the mornings, lazy cow. Had to kick her to the curb. She would still be in bed when I got home from work at 10 o'clock at night. If we can get her started, then we can go see my mate."

The Landrover was a decommissioned military vehicle, probably brought into Kenya by the British. The Loner, as she was known, was at least twenty-five years' old and had seen better days. It was named after the car from the Jim Carrey movie The Mask. The aluminum body shone through where the paint had been scratched off, there were dents in all the panels. The doors fitted where they touched, which was not often. The roof had been removed years ago. There were two rough, torn seats in the front the back had been converted to a flatbed. The 'Loner' stood brooding, challenging them to try to get her started. She just looked old and angry, like the lunatic bag lady dressed in multi-colored clothing on the street corner, shouting at all who passed by, ready to fight with anyone who catches her eye.

Jumping into the driver's seat Barry shouted, "Com'on, 'darlin', you know you want some, let's go for a little ride."

He pressed the start button, the ignition had disappeared years ago, to a dull thump as the starter lazily turned.

Barry started cajoling her, "Now that's no way to treat me, is it? Look, I've a guest here, don't embarrass me like this."

Again, he pumped the pedals, then gingerly pressed the button. This time it was worse, absolutely nothing happened. Brody laughed at the angry car and owner.

That was it for Barry. He was mad now, "Look, you bitch, I told you last time any more of this shit, and I am pushing you in the mangroves. I'll watch as the sea eats you up, every low tide I will come and kick your lazy ass."

Barry pressed the button over and over, shouting every time. The Loner just sat sullenly, slowly turning her engine.

He jumped out and said, "Sorry, mate, time to push."

Brody and Barry started pushing the Loner along the track. They managed to get the heavy Landrover to the top of a small rise. Then she was off down the other side, as if she was trying to get away from them. They chased after her down the hill. Barry jumped in the driver's seat, hammered the clutch to the floor, jammed her in second then slipped the clutch back up.

The Loner lurched as she caught. There was a massive belch of oily blue smoke from the exhaust as the huge, V8, normally aspirated engine burst into life. Once she was alive, it was like a rally car on drugs. The 200HP engine threw them along the tracks back towards town. The old 109 had leaf springs front and back. With very thin, worn padding left in the seats, every single pothole seemed like a massive crevasse in the road. The car leaped into them and then jarred on the opposite side, flying out towards the next hole. The doors constantly rattled, along with the bonnet and just about every other part of the vehicle. Barry shouted a running commentary all the way to the main road.

They hit the north-south artery and made a sharp right, heading out of town. The tarmac was not much better. Barry yelled, "This road was laid about ten years ago by the Chinese. It was good back then. But with all the bloody trucks and traffic, it's knackered now."

He was right. There were potholes everywhere, that and PikiPikis swerving in and out of the traffic. Plus big, black, old-fashioned, bicycles called black-mambas with men peddling and fat women dressed in colorful dresses, with huge sacks on their heads, perched on the rear luggage rack, chatting and shouting. This combined with the ever-present container trucks all heading north along this two-lane road. Barry continuously smashed the feeble horn as the old Landrover raced along the road, weaving between the dense traffic, trying to miss the deep potholes in the road.

As they drove, Barry explained. "Mate, we're off to Kikambala. It's a place up here a ways, in back off the main road."

They were speeding along the main road towards Malindi. It was still one lane north and one lane south with the big trucks dominating the whole width. Barry was weaving in and out of them whenever he saw a chance to overtake, either on the left or the right, he would floor the accelerator. The V8 petrol engine would roar, the air filters had long since been removed, and lunge forward, dragging the car along the road, like a small airplane running for takeoff.

Brody stared out of the windows of the Landrover. once they had left Mtwappa behind, the area became very rural very quickly. Just off the side of the road were small mud huts in groups, all with the same dried palm frond thatched roofs. Women pounded maize in large stone pots, using long wooden poles with rounded ends to crush the corn into a fine powder. Kids dressed in torn shirts and shorts were running around, chasing the dogs and goats or kicking a ball made from plastic bags and string. These children had no choice but to make their own toys from pieces of metal and wood, small carts they would push along in the dirt.

After about thirty minutes, Barry spoke. "Just up here, mate. We take a right and head into the bush a bit." Brody just smiled back, his voice hoarse from shouting, and his throat full of road dust.

They turned right after about another quarter of a mile, into a straight, dusty track lined with palm trees, heading almost due east back towards the ocean. On either side, there were smallholdings with goats and chickens wandering among the trees. The temperature was over 100 degrees, and the humidity here was at least 90%. With no shade, even the wind was like a hot wet blanket. Sweat poured down Brody's face into his eyes making them sting, the shirt he was wearing had dark shadows under his arms and down the back.

Barry slowed now that the track was becoming rougher. The rain had left high ridges, with grass growing on the top, leaving deep narrow ruts between. The car did not mind, this was what it had been built for.

The noise inside the vehicle reduced to a manageable roar. With the seats and doors rattling and the sound of the hardly muffled engine, it was like sitting in a boiling hot tractor.

They careered on down the track for what Brody guessed was about two miles, then hit a small river which crossed the road, making a deep muddy slash. Barry hardly slowed as he hit the water. The car went in roaring, charging straight through the deluge, she didn't even slow her pace as the stream sloshed in through the gaps under the doors. The wave from the car washed over the windscreen. The Loner relished this terrain and just carried on. Landrovers were specifically designed to be treated badly, and go on forever.

After another mile or so, they turned right then quickly right again along a deep-rutted, narrow road, enclosed by bushes and trees. Brody had no idea where Barry was taking him, but he seemed trustworthy enough, so he just hung in there for the ride. A few more minutes passed, then the car pulled to a sudden stop in front of a large black gate with a 9 feet high wall running off on both sides. Barry hooted twice. After what seemed like five minutes, a guard came and opened up for them, waving the growling vehicle through into a large compound. *Must be five acres in total* Brody thought to himself. The high wall ran all the way around the premises. Barry drove up to the front door and stopped the Loner. the silence was sudden and complete, one second there was so much noise now there was none. Brody sat for a moment. He could not hear a car, a kid, or a dog barking. It was strange, as if he was on another planet. The air was hot and stifling as the engine clinked away, starting to cool.

Barry turned and said, "So, mate, this is it. These are the guys a bit rough and ready, but they are OK once they know you are OK, if you know what I mean. This bunch loves the Muslim Prayers five times a bloody day I hear. First rule, trust them about as far as you can throw a camel. Second, don't make them mad!"

Brody nodded again, taking in the surroundings. This was certainly a remote place, he could only see the one guard on the gate, there were no dogs just a couple of chickens scraping in the dirt.

The house was about one hundred feet in length a single-storey block built building, with a roof made from palm fronds. Barry had pulled up in front of two enormous, ornately-carved wooden doors with birds and flowers all intertwined around the frame. Reaching back into the car, he blew the weak horn to announce their arrival. After what seemed like an age, the door creaked open. There was a boy of about sixteen or seventeen standing in the darkness. He was skinny and tall with a narrow face. His teeth were brown and crooked, on his head was a little turban type headdress, then the standard long white Kanzu covering his body. Brody immediately recognized him as a Somali. The inside of the house was shadowy keeping the heat of the day out.

The young boy said nothing, he just beckoned them into the house with a slight, weak wave.

Barry said. "Better take your shoes off, mate. These buggers don't like you wearing shoes indoors."

Brody complied, leaving their shoes in the dim hallway, and following the boy further into the complex. He noted to himself they had only seen one side. The house had three more, like a quadrangle, each independent of the other joined by narrow corridors. The boy led them from room to room in the cool house, finally opening a door into a courtyard at the center of the building. There was a huge mango tree growing from a small patch of earth in the middle of the yard, giving good shade. The temperature was very pleasant, even relaxing. Next to the mango tree was a small shallow pool about ten feet square, with a trickle of water from a fountain splashing into it. This seemed to cool the area even further.

Barry and Brody were offered seats next to the pond under the mango tree. Then hot, black, sweet tea was served. They drank in silence.

After waiting for what seemed like an hour, but was probably only ten minutes, time here appeared to move more slowly than the outside world, like an alternative universe where the hours are longer. Brody noticed a skinny, wiry figure in the shadows, the newcomer seemed to be hiding, not wanting his presence known, maybe assessing his new guests. Not wanting to be rude, Brody allowed the person his investigation without mentioning him to his partner. After a few more moments, the old man stepped out from one of the side rooms and approached, his bare feet padding almost silently over the flat paved courtyard. The old man was sure the two guys sat drinking tea had not noticed him until he was stood in front of the table. Barry immediately got to his feet and shook the small man's hand. Brody did the same. His hands were so soft they felt fragile, he seemed like a child, only his face was wrinkled and old with watery eyes peering out into the gloom. He had wisps of hair on his bald head and a few teeth when he smiled. The long Kanzu he was wearing was a dazzling white with intricate black embroidery around the collars and cuffs. After greeting the visitors, the man bade them sit, taking the chair on the opposite side of the table for himself. He said. "Barry, you bring us a visitor, this is so kind."

Barry replied, "Sir, he is a sailor like me. We met today. He asked for some particular items that I think you may be able to help with."

The old man said. "OK, but first let's introduce ourselves like civilized people. We are not animals here, we drink tea and chat to find who are friends are."

Barry said, "Sorry, my friend. I understand. This is Mr William Brody, he is staying with me in the bar. He has a dhow, and is sailing around Kenya and Tanzania enjoying your fine country."

The old man said with a slight smile, "Ah, this is not my country, this is Kenya. I am just a visitor for a while until my homeland can cool off."

Barry looked at Brody and said. "I must introduce you. This is Abdi Mohammed Mahmoud. He is from Somalia and Oman. He stays here for his peace and quiet, but he has connections all over the coast."

Brody stood formally, "It is great to meet you, Abdi. I am William Brody from the UK."

Abdi looked at Brody for a long moment, not saying a word, they just stood and stared at each other. Brody felt the sweat dripping down across his stomach as the old man surveyed him, as if he was thinking of what to do with him, like a snake watching a mouse, waiting patiently to attack.

The moment passed. Abdi said, "So, Mr Barry, what can we do for you both? I assume it is business we are doing here."

From then on, Abdi was all business and listened as Barry outlined his idea, "Brody here is in need of some firepower. You helped me, and I have now brought my friend as a customer. He travels the ocean, and we all know that is a dangerous place at times. I have advised him to get armed with at least something small to shoot the sharks when they try to eat him!"

Abdi nodded, "As always Barry, you are to the point. I believe the Australians are like that." Barry bristled, and said with a smile. "I'm a Kiwi mate, not an Aussie."

Abdi smiled back, showing his few remaining teeth, "My apologies, my friend. So, what did you have in mind for Mr Brody here?"

Barry said, "Well, what have you got to hand? We will need an AK, a small handgun, and we will have a look at whatever else you might have in the back store."

Abdi nodded and got to his feet. "Fine let's go and see what I have that is in working condition."

The three men walked towards the back of the house. When they were about three-quarters of the way through the building, Abdi turned down a side corridor. There were closed doors on either side of the barracks. It smelled of cooked cabbage and people, the dry, stale stench of a place recently used but empty now. There was easily enough space to house a small army.

Abdi slipped a key from inside his Kanzu into a secure metal door at the end of the corridor. Twisting the large black key in the lock, the door swung open on oiled hinges. As he stepped in, Brody noticed the soft, wet smell of gun oil. It hung in the air like a fog. The door had some sort of seal on the inside to prevent moisture. He could hear the whir of the air-conditioning. It was about fifteen degrees colder than outside. This was a special room.

Abdi walked to the wall and flicked a switch. Strip lights running along the center of the ceiling flickered and burst into life one by one. The room was about forty feet long and twenty feet wide with a cement floor, bare block walls, and a metal roof. Along each side of the wall and down the center of the room was row upon row of guns, cases of AK47's, the stock and trade of every African war or coup. Lining a dozen shelves were pistols of all sizes, some old, some looking brand new. In the center were several Strela shoulder-held surface to air missiles, and a row of shotguns, most old but in good condition.

Brody was impressed and let out a low whistle, "Abdi, this is quite an impressive display of armaments. Are you considering a war or what!"

Abdi Chuckled, "This is more a hobby than anything else. I'm just a collector of sorts."

Brody did not believe him for a minute, in his professional opinion he was looking at an armory that was ready for action. You could take the weapons directly out of here and go straight to the front line.

Abdi muttered, "You're a friend of Barry's. I know Barry and his bar and boat. We have been friends for many years now. Sometimes I help him and sometimes the other way around. We have an understanding he would only bring someone here who he trusted with my hobby."

Brody nodded his understanding. Abdi was making a clear threat to his new friend and his business. He had been shown the illegal weapons' cache, if word got out that Brody was anything other than what he claimed to be then Abdi would come looking for Barry. There was an implied debt now, and Brody knew if he breathed a word then, Barry would feel the consequences.

Brody looked along the lines of equipment. His fingers were itchy to touch and test each weapon, but he knew that would not be wise right now. He had to pick a couple of pieces and take it from there. His mind kept wandering back to the shoulder-held ground to air missiles. What the hell were they for? Those things cost a fortune, even on the black market and there were eight or ten stacked neatly in a row.

Brody asked, "What about ammunition, can you provide that as well?" Abdi smiled. "Show me what you want, and I will see if I can help you."

Brody picked a good but well-used AK47, the one with the fold-out stock. It was more versatile than the wooden stock, especially on a boat where the angles were tight, and there was likely to be close-quarter fighting. He then wandered along and picked from about a dozen Glock 17's. These pistols were great weapons. They rarely jammed and were easy to maintain. You could field strip it in seconds, then clean and reassemble. Brody could do this with the AK and Glock with his eyes closed in the dark!

A memory passed across his mind. An awful night in the D.R.C, during a long-protracted firefight. He had come across some rebels in a clearing. After emptying three mags into the group, the gun clicked empty. He had thrown his Glock at one of the attackers, slit his throat then grabbed his weapon. The gun was filthy, soaked from the rain. The guy had obviously been crawling through the thick mud. With rounds strafing around him, splinters flying from trees and flashbangs going off, he had stripped the gun down, and was just sliding it back together when a rebel charged out of the bush. A huge, broad-bladed knife came slashing out of the night. His training and reactions were all that saved him. His fingers slid the pieces together. He turned, putting two bullets in the rebel's face. The guys look of surprise as he died still haunted Brody's dreams.

Wandering along the row of weapons lost in thought, a perfect weapon for defending a small ship like his *Shukran* caught his eye. It was the last row at the far end of the room. He casually walked past it at first, picking up a long-barreled rifle. A sniper's weapon. Brody was a good shot but not a sniper. The weapon looked malevolent. There were two of them, evil sisters, laying on the shelf, looking like death itself. He admired the workmanship. they were Barrett Model 90s used for very long-distance sniper work. The bullet they fired was nearly half an inch across. these must have come off the container ships. Insurance companies had insisted on armed men traveling with the precious cargos recently, living on top of the stack of containers, and having one as a living space. The mercenaries would keep watch 24 hours a day as the ship cruised along the Somalian border. These guys loved to take target practice on anything that moved. The Barrett was the chosen weapon. Brody could not think how such specialized weapons had managed to find their way to a small armory shed in the middle of nowhere on the Kenyan Coast.

He put the long-barreled gun carefully back on the shelf, then started wandering back towards the door. Stopping as he passed a row of shotguns, casually picking one up to test the mechanism and feel the weight in his hands. The gun had been well looked after. There was a thin sheen of oil covering it, the mechanism was smooth but tight enough to know the gun was in excellent working condition. This was what he had been looking for all along. It was an Ithaca 37 twelve bore pump-action shotgun. The five-shot version with a pistol grip and no shoulder stock, perfect for close quarters if they were boarded.

Brody looked at it disdainfully, trying to put Abdi off the scent of a good profit, but carried it anyway, putting it on the table with the other two weapons. Abdi said, "Good choice, Mr Brody. I would have done the same if I was sailing a boat such as yours." Brody raised his eyebrows but said nothing.

They negotiated for a while, but Abdi did not seem that interested. The old man seemed happy with the $500.00 Brody offered for the lot. It was easy money. Anyway, all the weapons had been taken either from dead men or stolen from the army, so he was not too worried as it was all profit. For an extra $100.00, Abdi threw in a stack of ammunition for all the weapons, with spare magazines. The twelve bore shells came in a plastic bag from a supermarket!

Barry helped load the new purchases in the back of the Loner. She grumbled at them and would not start, so any 'street cred' they had built up in the negotiations was washed away. Abdi called the guard to help push-start the car down the rutted track.

Chapter Three

Brody woke on the second day to the *tap tap tap* of the 'Kalifati Fundi' below. *Shukran* was sat on the sand, propped up by the large wooden poles. The Fundi had said he would finish in the morning before the tide came. It was not yet light. There was a tinge of color on the horizon but still too dark to see.

Hassan had made coffee as usual, and there was a plate of mahamry, a small deep-fried cake the Swahilis eat for breakfast. Brody was eating his cake and sipping the sweet, scalding hot, dark coffee. The new weapons were safely stashed in the hold below his feet in a long, green, heavy-duty seaman's bag, he had bought in the market on the return journey with Barry. It gave him a good feeling to have some firepower. Now his crew were much safer. He would do some training later, then strip the guns, check all the parts, and stow them safely below decks, hopefully for good. Using them would be the last resort.

Swilling the last of the coffee down his throat, he quickly dressed in running shoes and shorts. It was time for the early morning session. This morning Brody felt unusually good. His guns made him feel more secure, and Wanjiku with her smile was always in his head. He sprinted along the sand, pushing himself harder than the day before. The marker tree was a surprise when he reached it. His breaths were labored, and his legs were sore with the exertion, but it felt like the right kind of pain. He turned and sprinted off back to *Shukran* at the same speed. When he arrived, the same as every day, Brody plunged off the side of the jetty, swimming out to the middle of the creek and then back in a fast, fluid freestyle stroke. His body was naturally fit. Having never visited a gym, he could not really see the point. Basic army training was all about using your body to get strong, running, jumping, press-ups. There was no real need to go to a special place and use machines. Swimming from a very early age and preferring freestyle over any other stroke had made his shoulders broad and very strong with long muscular arms. The army, of course, had seen this and taken it to the next level. After so many years of training, it was almost impossible for Brody to go a day without some strenuous physical activity. After the swim to the center of the creek, he climbed the ladder to the deck of his beached boat, then took a bucket of freshwater and poured it over his head. That was it, he was ready for a new day.

Brody went to find Hassan. He was under *Shukran*, chatting to the Fundi who was tapping his way along the hull. Hassan saw him coming. "Salam Alekum," Hassan and the Fundi said in unison.

Brody answered, "Habari Zenu," a greeting for more than one person. Now the greetings were over, they could get on with the conversations. Greetings were always imperative in Swahili and a must before anything could be done.

Hassan said, "Boss, it is all nearly done. My uncle here, or really second uncle. He is related to my father's brother through marriage. I have not seen him for many years."

Brody shook his hand firmly. The guy had massive shoulders and forearms from hammering and cutting all day, but skinny legs as these Fundis did all their work sitting down. He looked like a bodybuilder who had forgotten to work his lower legs.

The old man could not speak English, but explained anyway in Swahili to Brody. He chatted on, pointing at areas and tapping other areas with his hammer. Hassan was agreeing with the old sage. Brody listened intently, not understanding a word but not wanting to offend. He sipped his second coffee wondering exactly what was going on.

In the end, Hassan turned to Brody. "*Shukran* is in good condition. Most of the wood came from Tanzania and some from Lamu. The timber's not rotten. There are a few ribs inside which we will look at another day, but for now, my uncle says she is good to go!"

The crew had planned to antifoul *Shukran* in the morning, then get her into the water again. Gumbao rolled in at about 08:00. His new shorts were torn, and his shirt had a large bloodstain on the front. It looked like one of the parrots had been brutally murdered. Brody and Hassan ran over to him when he arrived on the beach. He was still smiling.

Hassan asked, "Bwana, what happened?"

Gumbao replied, "Ah, the checkers were not so good this time. Those Mtwappa guys they learn quick. I told them I was from the city and knew the rules better. I used my old trick, when I get a King I can bring a new piece back, and then I said if I jump you I get another go. It was working fine, I was winning again. Then some smart ass from Nairobi came and told them I was lying. Haki A Mungu! They got mad. I escaped with my life."

He did not seem too worse for wear. His clothes were back to normal. Just another day in his life. He just got on with his work, back to square one again.

The antifouling was painted on three coats thick, finishing just as the water was coming. They applied the last strokes before pushing *Shukran* off the poles and back out into the creek.

Hassan hurried around *Shukran* looking for leaks. Either new ones or the old ones which had not been filled correctly. This was a wooden vessel which had been repaired pretty much constantly since she was launched some twenty or thirty years ago. A dhow is always just getting ready to sink, and is patched up here and there with anything you have at hand, Meaning the structural integrity of the boat was doubtful, to say the least. As she went through the waves, the water would twist the craft like a corkscrew back and forwards, the planks sliding against each other, creaking and groaning as she sailed through the long Indian Ocean swells. To have her out on dry land was dangerous. The weight of the superstructure on the keel without the support of the water around the hull could cause planks to loosen or shift. But the Fundi had done his work, and all was well for now.

Brody stood on the stern deck in the afternoon sunshine, surveying his beautiful boat. While he had been in Mombasa with Hassan and Gumbao, they had decided to spend some of the money from the diamonds. It was burning a big hole in their pockets. After lengthy discussions in a back-street coffee shop, it was finally agreed. Gumbao wanted some new parts and tools for the engine. Hassan had asked for cooking equipment, ropes, and a new sail. Brody had decided he wanted some navigation equipment. Most of the stuff was easy to find in the Old Town of Mombasa. Gumbao knew the streets from when he was a child. He had been left outside an orphanage in the Old Town as a tiny baby, Then grew up on the streets hustling his way through, stealing food and being chased by the cops. It was only one day when he was down looking for opportunities at the docks when a fisherman had grabbed him as crew on his boat. He was lucky and had managed to get off the streets before it was too late. Drugs were constantly killing the street children of the town.

The navigation equipment was harder to find. They had to locate the big chandlery warehouses that catered to the larger ships. After several hours of trudging up and down in the boiling, busy streets, the eclectic group found an Indian shop, way off the beaten track. They entered the darkness to find an enormously fat Indian sat behind a desk on the other side of a three-foot-wide counter. The shop looked like it had been robbed. There was stuff everywhere from floor to ceiling in piles. The shelves had random spanners, ropes, screwdrivers, winches and all manner of items stacked this way and that. Brody immediately lost hope. This was just a dumping ground, another dead end. He was about to give up completely. Then the fat Indian looked up from his papers and in perfect English said. "Good afternoon, sir, how may we be of assistance?"

As always, Brody replied politely, "We are looking for electronic navigation systems, with a through the hull depth sounder, and GPS with maps of the coast."

The Indian looked thoughtful for a moment, then said, "Do you require radar or is it just the GPS?"

Brody was shocked at this, "Radar would be great if you have it."

The Indian rattled off some instructions in Gujarat to one of his employees, who immediately ran off into the back of the store.

He then turned to Hassan, speaking in fast, fluent Swahili, asking him a series of questions. Brody only guessed what was going on, but the guy seemed to want to know about the type of boat they were using.

Then the Indian turned back to Brody and continued, "Please take a seat. I will have something for you in a few moments. Have some tea, it is fresh."

After about fifteen minutes, two guys came back from the warehouse carrying six large boxes. They triumphantly piled them up in front of the worn and scarred wooden desk.

The Indian called Brody over and said, "Currently, with your requirements and your dhow, I would advise this system. It is the Lowrance HDS 10, full-blown."

The fat, helpful Indian went through all of the pros and cons of the HDS units. Brody was shocked at the knowledge of the old guy sat in front of him. After another hour and a half, the crew were the proud owners of a full set of equipment including Radar and maps for the whole of the East African Coast.

For a bottle of expensive rum, Barry had agreed to come on board and help set up the equipment. The HDS 10 was a great bit of kit. It had a twelve-inch color screen, full maps of the coast from Mozambique to the Horn of Africa. Brody had added a 3KW through-hull transducer and side-scan sonar for good measure. The transducer would give a clear picture of the bottom to eight hundred feet, way more than was needed, but good to have. The side-scan sonar allowed them to spot good diving reefs without driving over the top, especially good in shallow water. He was very happy with the equipment. They would now know their exact position at all times, and have eyes at night if they had to enter a port.

At around 15:00 after successfully re-launching *Shukran* off the beach, she was back alongside the jetty, next to the Full Moon. Brody was sat in the stern cabin, enjoying a cold Tusker. Barry shouted from the shore, "Permission to come aboard!"

Brody replied, "Welcome aboard." He then got up and started pouring a double rum with ice.

Barry had sailed the oceans on his own for over ten years before arriving in Mtwappa. He had learned how to survive at sea and had become quite a 'Fundi' when it came to installing and repairing marine equipment. Most sailors learn very quickly. There is no repair guy two hundred miles offshore, and no hardware store around the corner, so they become very self-sufficient.

Brody watched carefully as Barry slowly emptied the bottle of rum while expertly installing the equipment. The through-hull transducer took a while. Finding a suitable place on the hull was a little tricky, but after some work and rearranging, they were able to fit the black, rectangular box and screw it down securely. As *Shukran* was a fat-bellied dhow, her first planks coming off the keel were very broad, about 14" and almost flat. It was relatively easy to get the electronic box lying correctly against the wood.

Brody got into his dive equipment, jumped off the side of *Shukran*, then worked below, fitting the side-scan sonar, just in front of the propeller out of the wash. The electronic box had to be screwed tightly to the hull in an out of the way place with no obstructions. The crew would then be able to see reefs to the side of the boat as well as below.

The radar was last to go on top of the stern cabin. They achieved this with the help of Gumbao and Hassan, as Barry was having difficulty standing up at this point. However, once it was finished, Barry turned it all on, set the calibrations, and watched as the radar picked the solid structures around them, showing them clearly on the electronic map. Then he split the screen. It now showed the coastline on one side and the depth of the water in a long blue column on the other. Any debris which a sonar pulse could bounce off showed up as small green fish.

At daybreak the next morning, it was all-hands-on-deck. Brody had banned Gumbao from leaving *Shukran* the night before, they had eaten and slept early.

The whole crew were wide awake long before the sun started working its hot way up the side of the sky. They untied in the pitch darkness of a tropical night. He used the instruments to slowly motor out towards the open ocean. The crew had decided the night before to conduct sea trials, testing the ship after all the work and to get used to the new instruments. The radar clearly showed the twisting creek in the darkness. The red screen was constantly reading the depth of the water below the hull. The map had a small line of dots, a breadcrumb trail, showing the safest way out of the harbor and creek. Motoring slowly along, watching for fishermen in the dugout canoes which would not show up on the radar, as they were made of wood, skin, and bones.

Gumbao took lookout in the bow. Hassan was on the wheel and Brody was giving directions with the new machine. Their craft slowly approached the surf line on the final leg before entering the Indian Ocean. *Shukran* started moving with the swells, lifting, and dropping, cruising between the breakers. Dawn was slowly arriving in the east, at first a faint glow appearing then rising quickly out of the ocean, laying a golden glittering path across the water. *Shukran* sailed straight out of the mouth of the entrance, following the glittering path towards the sun. The wind was from the northeast, the 'Kaskazi,' in Swahili. Gumbao and Brody hauled the heavy boom to the top of the mast, tugged the sheet to release the sail, tying it off on the sternpost. With the engine off, the crew sat back to enjoy the peace of the ocean and swell of the waves as *Shukran* carried them offshore. Their heading was almost east with a hint of north. The current at this time of year was heading from the south to the north so they would be dragged even further along the coast.

The crew settled in and sailed in silence for over an hour. Once they were in the open ocean, Brody took the wheel as Hassan looked for leaks. He scoured the hold from bow to stern, checking planks and ribs looking for any potential problems. He came up from below smiling and reported to Brody that all was well.

They continued into the morning, traveling at 6 knots, slowly pacing through the water. Gumbao set about running some lines from the stern. During their stay in Mombasa, they had picked up two tuna rods from a very enthusiastic guy in a local fishing shop.

Brody had been impressed with his knowledge of fishing and learned a considerable amount in the short discussion they had. The guy was called Lauren and had lived on the coast in Kenya his whole life. His passion was deep-sea fishing.

Brody asked, "Listen, I want to fish off the back of a dhow. What do you recommend?"

Lauren thought for a moment. "This is quite unusual. Most of our stuff is for engine boats. You have more control over what is happening."

Brody was listening intently, getting as much information as possible, almost like interrogating a prisoner of war but without the waterboarding! "That's the challenge. We need something compact, and strong. I free diver with my speargun, I think the fight should be evenly matched."

Lauren smiled at this. "You are my kind of fisherman. I think the short, dumpy, tuna rods are the best option for you. We can run them with lightweight tackle. They do not whip and bend like most rods, you get a real feel for the fish. The line is lighter too, so if you mess up, the fish breaks the line and wins the day!"

This sat well with Brody. It was not like he was fishing for a living. There had to be some competition in the game. "So, let's have a look at what you have to offer, Lauren. I can see we are like-minded."

Lauren showed Brody an array of rods and reels, giving his special advice for each one. "These smaller reels are called thirty pounders. We use monofilament 30 lb. line. It's strong but a decent billfish can break it like cotton. You have to cajole the fish in like a lady, gradually getting her closer and closer." Lauren had a far off look in his eye. Brody could tell he was reliving some great fishing moment.

Brody said, "That sounds great. Let's have two then with these nice reels. Chuck in the line and I will have some of those billfish and tuna lures too." The lures, hanging on the display, looked like brightly colored fish but hidden inside were two deadly looking stainless steel barbed hooks.

As Brody left the shop, Lauren said, "Tight lines. This time of year you get all sorts out there. The big five we call them, marlins, stripey, black and blue, sailfish, and at night even swordfish."

Brody said, "Thanks," then waved and left with his new haul.

That had been a week ago. Now the crew were all keen to try out these new rods to see if Lauren was right.

Gumbao let the lines out behind the boat, one on the port and one on the starboard side. *Shukran* was moving at about 6 knots, which was a bit slow for trawling, but you never knew what was hanging about. Once the lines had been set to his satisfaction, he came to Brody. "Hey boss, you watch the rods. I will take the wheel." Gumbao knew more about sailing than fishing with this new equipment.

Brody sat on the rear gunwale, his feet dangling over the side, staring out into the white wake flowing out behind them. She was cantered over slightly to the starboard side as the wind pushed them along. It was almost silent, just the breeze blowing through the rigging and the offshore birds circling above, crying to each other, waiting to see if any fish got stirred up. The boat sailed onwards into the early morning sun. Following the slight blue-green swells of the ocean, moving in a rhythmic beat, slowly lifting and dropping the bow of *Shukran* letting the stern follow through on the long unbroken waves.

Abdi Mohammed Mahmoud listened to the cleric singing the last of the prayer from the front of the mosque. This was Abdi's mosque, built in the grounds of his secure compound in Kikambala just north of Mtwappa. Raising his head as the prayer finished, saying, "Allah Akbar, Allah Akbar," aloud to bless the Holy Mohammed, then rising slowly to his feet. Abdi was an old man but had prayed five times a day since he had been six years old. He knew the Koran well. He knew the Koran was written for men like him.

Leaving the mosque for the short walk to his house, he came across Muna his old friend of forty years. They had fought together in Somalia against the Ethiopians and Muzungus. The two friends had escaped to Kenya, several years ago, for some peace and time to plot. Muna greeted him, "Salaam Alekum, Mzee."

Abdi replied, "Alekum Salaam, Muna." With the pleasantries, which were so important in their social world, over they could continue.

Abdi said, "These 'Muzungus', they all have the watches and the clocks, and they have their stupid calendar run off the sun. Who would think to use the sun when the moon gives you so much more information?"

Muna agreed, "They are a young people that believe they know everything. As you say, they have the watches but we have the time. We can wait and strike when we feel it is best, then disappear and wait and strike again as we please."

Abdi spoke, "How are the plans moving my friend?"

Muna replied, "We are on time, Inshallah." 'God be willing.'

Abdi waited a moment to let the silence sink into their conversation. His people were not like the 'Muzungus'. They still appreciated the gaps as much as the talking part, not just waiting for the other to finish speaking, just to start again. There was pace and pleasure, time to enjoy the company.

Abdi went on, "We must not fail this mission. The eyes of the world will be focused on us. Our new partners will be watching our every move. When do you meet with them?"

Muna replied, "Our new friends have already landed up north in Wajir. The group are traveling down today. I will meet them tomorrow or maybe the next day. Our new partners are in a hurry for this to happen. They say it must happen on the Jew Holiday for maximum effect."

Abdi thought again for a moment, taking his time, letting the information sink in, "This is good news. Together we can defeat all the infidels, Christians, and Jews."

Abdi left him and went towards the large house. Muna had a huge smile on his face as he walked purposefully towards the small Toyota Corolla parked near the gate. The passenger side door was opened by his long-time driver and confidant, Adib. Muna said. "A good day, Adib. We will be famous very soon. The righteous will stand and Allah's name will be written in blood across the world."

Adib smiled at the thought. He had been with Mzee Muna for over twenty years, working beside him, watching his dream grow. He said, "Mzee this is a good day. Blessed be Allah, Inshallah,"

They drove off along the rough track back towards Mombasa old town.

Brody had been watching the lines, but the soft rocking of the boat going through the swells combined with the sound of the water running against the hull as it washed past them had lulled him into a meditative state. It took him a second to register as Hassan shouted, "Hey, Boss, the reel! The reel!"

He snapped out of the dream instantly to the sound of the screaming reel on the port side. The line was shedding off at an incredible rate. The ratchet on the reel was racing as the line was pulled, letting out a high-pitched whine as it spun.

Hassan said, "Boss, take the reel quickly!" then darted over to the starboard side and started frantically winding the other line in so there would be no tangles in the water.

Gumbao shouted urgently," Boss, hi ni Samaki kubwa sana." 'That's a big fish.' He then concentrated on keeping *Shukran* on a steady course.

Fishing off a sailboat was entirely different from fishing off a vessel with an engine. For starters, you do not have reverse, you can only sail the points of the wind. Maneuvering was a whole different ball game.

Brody stood with the rod held high behind the boat, the butt end jammed between his legs as he slowly increased the brake, ever wary that if he tightened too quickly, the line could snap, letting the prized fish go free, along with the new shiny lure and expensive hooks. He settled in for the fight. This was going to be fast and hard and he could easily lose this battle with the line breaking or the fish spitting the hook out.

Suddenly, the line went slack. Brody quickly reeled in as fast as he could. The fish was coming to the surface. Keeping the tension as tight as possible was imperative as the fish raced back from the depths. His left thumb moved left to right as the line came in, ensuring it laid evenly into the reel. The fish burst from the ocean about one hundred and sixty feet away from the boat. Its green, shimmering body with, flat, block-like head flew into the air almost fifteen feet. It shook, its head from side to side, angrily trying to spit the razor-sharp hooks out of its mouth. It was truly a sight to behold, a massive bull dorado or dolphin fish. Its beautiful, bright green body covered in small black spots with a white underbelly. These fish hunted the smaller creatures that live along the weed lines or around any floating debris in the ocean.

The fish dived again, trying to break free. Brody had gained a lot of line as the fish had come to the surface, but now he felt the line stripping out again heading for the depths. The dorado didn't go as deep this time and started to surface. Brody hauled in the line as fast as he could. He was sweating in the morning sun; his thighs felt like they were on fire as the incredible strength of this forty-pound muscle fish just pulled and pulled.

Brody kept winding in as the fish leapt for a second time. He waved his enormous head as before, but the stainless-steel hooks could not be dislodged. The dorado hit the water, and raced away from the boat. The beautiful, lime green fish swam in an arc from port to starboard at the stern of *Shukran*. Gumbao sensed the fish was losing spirit, so he brought her into the wind to slow her down. The loose sail started to flap. The dorado zigzagged from port to starboard in the flat ocean. Taking some line here and there, but Brody, although he felt like he had done a forced march through the Brecon Beacons in Wales, was winning.

The fish swam close to the boat to try to loosen the hooks rammed into the hard palate of its mouth. But Brody kept the line tight, pulling it closer to the stainless steel sharpened hook in Hassan's hand. Then the bull dorado went straight down with all of its strength peeling line off the reel. Brody could only watch as all of his hard work was now spewing back into the ocean, yard by yard.

The huge fish turned at about one hundred feet. Brody felt the turn as all the tension released from the line. He reeled as fast as the reel would go, a desperate fight against time. The gears in the hub of the small reel were hot from all the line coming in and out.

Brody shouted, "Hassan, the gaff! Get the gaff ready on the port side! Gumbao, keep her into the wind, this monster is tired!"

The fish surfaced about thirty feet from the side of *Shukran*. It was exhausted. Brody's arms were like jelly as he slowly reeled the big bull over to the boat. Hassan reached in and expertly gaffed the fish, bringing it on deck where it started fighting all over again. It was only over when Gumbao moved across the boat and put it out of its misery with several swift blows to its skull. They quickly put the large fish into the cooler box so it would not spoil. It meant they had fish now for many days ahead.

As *Shukran* was sitting into the wind, they forced the boom onto the other tack and settled themselves down for the return journey to the beach. Brody was thinking of cold beer.

After two hours of sailing, they approached the coast about six miles further north of Mtwappa.

Gumbao expertly turned *Shukran* to start a short, dead run to bring her to the main entrance to the small inlet leading to the mooring at the Full Moon Bar, and a cold beer.

Brody was staring at the white beaches along the coast. "Hassan, which hotels are these?" There were many hotels with sunbeds the other side of the reef with people playing on the sand, enjoying the afternoon sun.

Hassan started reeling them off, "That is Africa Beach, then you have the Continental." He pointed to a long-roofed building, "Then you have Leopard Beach hotel where my cousin works, that's the Peponi Hotel."

Brody gazed at the long white broken surf line carrying on all the way to Mtwappa, then the stretch of flatwater showing the entrance. The new Lowrance HDS10 was methodically plotting the ocean floor. As the water quickly became shallower, the reef and fish were appearing on the screen as large black lumps, with crazy little hovering green fish above them. Under one hundred feet was a good dive range. He could plot some points to return to later. *Shukran* was moving at four and a half knots through the waves. The current was against them pushing them back towards the north, fighting the wind in the sail. They passed over some small rocky outcrops on the bottom, then suddenly the thick black line mapping the seabed started heading for the surface, almost vertically, a cliff face underwater. The line turned ninety degrees at sixty feet. There were hundreds of little green fish appearing as the depth finder's sonar bounced off the small creatures above the reef. It ran for about four hundred feet before dropping off again, a large lump of rock sticking out of the ocean bottom. Brody marked it with the built-in GPS. This would be worth investigating at a later date. He looked up and could see the Peponi Hotel on the beach in a deadline of sight, directly east of their current position.

Another hour and a half slowly passed before *Shukran* approached the inlet. The engine was started, the sail pulled down and tightly wrapped against the lowered boom. The crew readied her for the mooring, ropes were brought on deck, fenders were tied to the running rail as the boat slowly motored along the creek. Ten minutes later, they were safely tied up alongside the Full Moon Bar.

Brody left Hassan to clean the fish and start preparing their late lunch of dorado and ugali. Gumbao was checking the engine below to make sure it had not suffered during the journey.

Brody headed for the bar. Barry was perched on a high stool. "Gooday, mate, how was the sailing?" Barry started with his usual cheerful attitude.

Brody answered, "It was good, got a nice dorado for lunch and the equipment works great, thanks."

Barry smiled as he waved the bartender over, "Here, mate, get this guy a drink and a refill for me."

Brody took the bottle of ice-cold beer, gratefully taking a long pull on the bottle, then asked, "Those guys from yesterday, should I be worried about them,"

Barry answered with raised eyebrows, "No, mate, as long as you don't rat on them or they think you ratted on them, you should be fine."

Brody just smiled back.

After an hour and a quick lunch, he headed back towards town, finding one of the PikiPikis on the road and paying for the one-way trip to the center of Mtwappa. He was dropped off on the busy, dust and diesel fumed main street. It did not matter when you arrived in this town, it was always full on, 24 hours a day seven days a week. The trucks never stopped rumbling north full and returning south empty for the refill. This was the only road from Mombasa port, the deepest port in East Africa, to South Sudan, Ethiopia, and Somalia.

Brody wandered through the lively market for a while, enjoying the sights and smells of Africa. Dried fish hanging from colored string by the side of the road, the brightly colored wraps the Swahili wear around their waist all out on display. It was a different world, loud, noisy, and brash.

He was walking along a side street eating a samosa, when he heard from behind him, "That's probably donkey you are eating. I did warn you."

Brody laughed. He knew that voice. He turned. Sure enough, standing behind him wearing a short denim miniskirt, and a black T-Shirt, with 'Vogue' plastered across the chest in bright fake pearls, was Wanjiku.

She smiled that smile with all of those bright white teeth. Her hair had changed, to about half the length and was dead straight which Brody thought weird.

He said, "Hi. I was going to come find you later, but wanted to have a look around first."

Wanjiku smiled again. "Great, you can take me to the bar and buy me lunch."

Brody agreed without a second thought.

They went to Wanjiku's dad's bar behind her mother's beauty shop. As Brody walked through, he could feel all of the ladies' eyes on him. He noticed Wanjiku wiggle her butt a bit more in that tight skirt, her broad smile growing as she saw the envious looks from the other ladies having their hair done.

They sat and had a cold Tusker each. Wanjiku said, "So what you been up to?"

Brody answered, "Just fixing the boat a bit and fishing. Nothing much."

"But you have been out to Kikambala with Barry," She said slyly.

Brody laughed, "How do you know that?"

Wanjiku replied, "Ah, Bwana. This is Africa. I know your every move from the morning you wake until you finish drinking there with Barry in the evening." She winked at him. "We keep our eye on everything."

Brody was impressed with her surveillance techniques. She had probably not just bumped into him in the market either!

Wanjiku asked, "What were you doing out in Kikambala? There are people in this place it is better not to know."

Brody said, "Who would that be?"

She looked him in the eye. Her smile was gone, "Some people are only here to cause trouble. We don't agree with them, but they are powerful, and have friends in the government. Some are dangerous too. Be careful, Mr Brody, white guys can just disappear from here and never be seen again."

Brody was touched she was trying to help him.

Then Mr Mwangi came in, carrying a large box. He spotted Brody and diverted immediately to the kitchen, in a hurry. Wanjiku laughed, "Father has been out, finding things again. He does not want you to see!"

They continued with their lunch of fried chicken, and mokimo, a Kikuyu dish of mashed potatoes, maize, and peas.

Wanjiku's father appeared as they were finishing the meal. He had a slick salesman's grin on his face, starting his pitch with, "Hey, Mr Brody, how do you communicate with the land when you are out in the ocean?"

Brody had not really thought about it before, there was no one to communicate with anyway!

He replied, "We don't really. We just land at the beach or port when we need something."

Wanjiku's father was ready. "Ah, Mr Brody, that is not safe. You never know when you might need to call Wanjiku." He winked at Brody then went on. "Or you might need to call for help. It would be terrible to be lost in the ocean without being able to call for assistance."

Wanjiku interrupted, "Dad, what are you up to?"

Wanjiku's father smiled and said, "I am only trying to look after your new 'Muzungu.' we don't want him getting lost. You have been running all over town checking on him these last few days." He said with a wicked grin on his face.

Wanjiku blushed and slapped her father, "Dad, what are you after here? Brody is our guest!"

Mwangi said importantly, "I happen to have a friend in the new telecommunications industry. He says it is the next thing in Kenya. Everyone will have a phone in their pocket." He laughed at the idea. "Imagine, in your pocket."

Mwangi went on, "He has offered me a few at a very special price. An opening deal, if your new friend here buys one then he gives me the second one free. I will give it to you, Wanjiku."

Brody smiled. This was the punch line he had been waiting for.

Brody asked, "How much for one Mr Mwangi?"

Mwangi replied, "For you Mr Brody just $450.00. It's brand new and even in the box!"

Brody looked at them both standing in front of him, the most innocent people he had ever seen!

"I will give you $200.00 for the phone. That's all I have right now so I can't go higher."

Mwangi looked crestfallen as if Brody had slapped him in the face, "Ah, Bwana, you can't do that I have to at least cover my costs. Give me $400.00 and we can seal the deal now with a cold drink." He was reaching behind the bar for the bottles, Brody held up his hand and said. "OK. my final offer is 300."

Mwangi shot his hand out and shook Brody's for a second then replaced it with a cold Tusker.

Mwangi let Brody drink his beer, then stood waiting and fidgeting. "Our deal is over now, I must go and pay for the phones quickly before they are all gone."

Brody smiled, he knew this was all a game. He handed over three one hundred dollar bills from this back pocket.

In about thirty minutes, Mwangi was back. His shoulders were stooped, and his brows were furrowed. He came straight into the bar and said, "Look, Bwana, the telephone guy has given me the phones," He handed Brody two silver flip-open phones and some chargers.

Brody said, "And the boxes, I thought they were new?"

Mwangi said, "Ah, well, that was earlier this is all he had left. We were lucky to get these, they work for sure, and they're good."

Brody smiled, shrugging his shoulders. This was not the first time he had been taken, nor, he was sure, would it be the last. This was Africa, nothing was ever as it was painted. He thought he was buying two new mobile phones and now he had two very second-hand ones.

The deal brought back memories, and a smile, from his days in Zimbabwe training the special forces units. Then fighting alongside them in the bush against the rebel forces. The young recruits were rough and ready. Most had come from massive 50 thousand acre ranches scattered across the county. Whenever a situation occurred that was just plain odd or out of their control, one of the guys would say. "Hey, T.I.A."

Brody asked them what it meant. The lad's explanation was. "Bro, this is Africa, you can never see the logic or understand why some stuff happens. It just does, so we say. T.I.A. This is Africa!"

Brody thought to himself as he took a long pull on his cold Tusker. *T.I.A!*

Chapter Four

The six young guys got off the small Cessna 208 Caravan. Their limbs were stiff after traveling nonstop for nearly twelve hours, leaving the outskirts of Palestine in the early hours of the morning almost a day ago crammed into a small white delivery van with Aviation Supplies painted on the side in large black letters, sitting uncomfortably on the bare metal wheel arches of the truck as it rattled along the dusty roads heading for the small town of Khan Unis. If there had been windows, they would have seen the lights of the town pass them by. Then the Unwra Refugee camp glowing in the distance, a place that never slept.

The soldiers sat silently in the back of the truck. The driver had been well paid to deliver them safely to their destination. But there were always risks in these circumstances. Someone could pay more.

The van lurched to a stop. The group heard voices outside, then the sound of a gate grinding on a dirt and stone-littered roadway, then moving off again, slower now. The road was rough, full of potholes or they may have been driving across a rough open space. The young men bounced around, falling against the sides of the panel truck as it wound its way. The vehicle plowed straight across the space. Their heads hit the roof as it hit a hard ridge, throwing them back against the door. Then it was smooth again. They were back on tarmac. The van glided along the even surface for a few more moments, then came to a gentle stop. The six men waited in silence. Their country was hot, and the panel van was hot even at this ungodly hour in the morning. They sat in the darkness, listening and waiting patiently for the doors to open, with glistening faces, shirts stuck to their backs.

Finally, they heard footsteps approaching, keys jingling on a ring in someone's hand. The lock was turning and one door was pulled open, then the other. The group gratefully stepped out into the hot, humid night. This country never knew the cold. It did not matter which season you were in it was either hot or hotter.

Standing on the tarmac, their eyes slowly adjusted to the early morning gray. The sun would be up in an hour or so, burning this place without mercy as it did each day.

There were two men: the driver of the truck who was anxious to leave, and a new guy with a pair of mirror Rayban sunglasses in his hand. His white shirt was neatly pressed, he had dark maroon trousers and shiny, slip-on, comfortable shoes. The leader of the group guessed this was Salim Afrad, their captain for the flight. He looked them over, then motioned them to the plane.

Salim had been there most of the night, he had been well paid for this trip. But everything considered, the price was fair. It was a long, arduous journey, some two thousand three hundred miles across open, desolate, barren, unpopulated country. He always took his job seriously, but with his current passengers, he had been warned to double and triple check the plane and route. There could be no hiccups without serious repercussions. His Cessna 208 turboprop was a fine aircraft, very reliable. He had used them since arriving in North Africa some fourteen years ago. She could take up to 9 passengers, 12 if he threw the seats out. Salim had arrived at the small airstrip many hours earlier, personally monitoring the fueling, then making sure the tank was topped off to the maximum; three hundred and thirty-five and one-half gallons of the best aviation fuel he could lay his hands on.

He loved his plane and his life even more so, never taking any unnecessary chances. The voice on the telephone had assured him all the flight plans were cleared out of Palestine. The voice had sent the call signals over with a courier. No return address. Salim just hoped these guys were competent. Everything so far had been professional and secretive, even the money had arrived in cash. No paper trail.

Salim would fly this flight solo, no second in command. This had been the first stipulation of the verbal contract. Nobody involved that was not absolutely essential to the deal. It was good news for Salim. He did not have to share his pile of new American one hundred dollar bills.

The pilot made sure his six passengers were safely strapped in, then got comfortable in his seat setting the controls for takeoff. Finally, after all, preflight checks had been done, he began taxiing out to the end of the runway without calling to the tower which was dark at this hour anyway. The airport was closed. He increased the engine speed until it was growling like a caged animal. Releasing the brakes, the plane slowly moved along the flat black tarmac. The Cessna quickly caught speed and within seconds was racing towards the end of the strip. They did not even reach halfway before the plane took to the air and soared away to the southwest.

The route he was taking had been planned by his employer. It took them over the desolate territory of the Sahara Desert for the most part. This was a place you could just disappear into. The first leg of the journey was just over one thousand miles at twenty thousand feet. The nomads walking across the hot sand with their camels in a long single file, a stark contrast to the barren yellow desert all around them, did not even notice the faint vapor trail high above them in the clear blue sky.

The Cessna cruised along at two hundred miles an hour. Their first refueling point was just over five hours away.

The passengers sat dozing in their seats in the rear as the plane leveled off and droned on its route into the desert. The only one awake was Malik. He had been chosen by his father to lead this group of six to head the mission to Kenya. Abdi, the Muslim from Somalia, had visited them on several occasions in Palestine. They had similar beliefs. Malik's father had entrusted this important mission to his eldest son. The burden was heavy but worth it. They had planned for months, meticulously working out every detail. Malik and his five followers were trained as urban guerrillas and were at the peak of fitness, ready and willing to strike a blow in the name of Allah against the Christians and the Jews. A double blow which would bring the world to its knees.

The Cessna 208 flew on, chewing up the miles as they crossed the deserted, flat, sandy plains below. As the sun was hitting its zenith, the plane started its slow descent. The group were heading for a private airfield one hundred and twenty miles south of Khartoum. The pilot had exact GPS coordinates of the small strip, but he could see it from about fifteen miles away. The area had been cleared from the sands around it. The runway could easily be seen from the air a much darker straight yellow line running north to south with a small hut at one end and a limp windsock hanging in the boiling sun.

The pilot expertly approached and touched down just after noon, then taxied to the end of the runway next to the small stone building. The engine was finally switched off. Suddenly, the silence of the desert surrounded them. As the doors opened, a blast of hot, dry air hit them taking their breaths away. The young soldiers had worked in the heat of their home country for many years. But this was different. This was real desert heat, too hot to even sweat. The air stole the water as it leaked from their pores, not giving it a chance to help cool their bodies, like the blast from a steel smelting furnace. Stumbling out onto the hard-packed earth, they already regretted leaving their seats and the comfort of the air-conditioned cabin. The soldiers stretched their cramped bodies for a second to get the circulation running. The door of the hut opened and a man covered in black from head to toe came out and stared at them.

He looked at the pilot, "Wait for fuel one hour." He then went back into his hut and shut the door. The group huddled under the wings of the aircraft, trying to get into some shade in the incredible heat as the long, slow minutes ticked by.

After one and a half hours, a dust trail appeared on the horizon. It was silent, just zigzagging across the barren uneven desert towards them. When it was close enough to see the truck ahead of the huge dust plume, they could hear the grinding of the gears as the heavy fully-laden flatbed worked its way across the soft sands, then the hard rock towards them. The truck drove across the final rough tracks and desert, arriving at the end of the runway next to the sagging windsock. It was an ancient Ford pick-up. It must have been twenty-five years old and full of holes, the sand had worn most of the paint off the vehicle. On the flatbed behind the driver was a fuel bowser. The cabin was blaring music from the bazaars which echoed around the empty landscape. A tall skinny Arab got out of the truck, dressed in black from head to toe, his head and faced covered. There were no greetings or handshakes, just a nod from the pilot and a nod from the driver.

Thirty minutes later, the fuel had been tested and the tank filled. The group gratefully piled back into their seats as the engine burst into life, pouring cold air down onto their heads. The plane quickly taxied to the runway, then raced up into the picture-perfect blue sky for the second long haul of the flight.

After taking off, the group were now faced with another six hours of flying over barren and desolate, land. The wasteland went on forever, not a town or village in sight. It was as if they were entirely alone on an abandoned planet. The pilot had noted they had not been called once on the radio but this changed as they came to the Kenyan border.

Suddenly, the plane was full of noise as the Kenyan radar picked them up. The voice of a tower control came blasting into the cockpit.

"This is Nairobi Tower Control. Aircraft heading due east on route to Wajir, identify yourself." The pilot calmly read out the instructions he had been given. "This is Six Two Niner, Cessna 208, U.N. Number Eight Sixty-Four."

Tower Control Came Back, "Please state landing airport and nature of business."

Salim replied, "This is Air Ambulance, SIX TWO NINER on route to Wajir. We have an international patient to pick-up at Wajir Airport."

There was some discussing at the other end. The Kenyan Tower Control then said, "All clear to continue for Wajir Airport."

Salim wiped a line of sweat from his brow. That had been the most nerve-wracking part of the journey so far but the right palms had been greased. The plan was working well.

They touched down on the dry, brown earth of Wajir International Airport, taxiing over to the far south-eastern corner where a small car was waiting for them. Once the engines had stopped and were silent, the captain opened the door and was met by a fat-bellied, sweating, customs official. He had a stamp pad and pen ready. Malik handed the passports his father had given him to the officer. He waddled back to his car for a few minutes and came back holding six, sweat covered, passports duly stamped and processed.

Malik breathed a sigh of relief. His soldiers were over the first and maybe the most dangerous part of the journey.

A big white V8 Toyota Landcruiser with dark tinted windows pulled up after about thirty minutes, once the customs officer had left. The driver went straight out of the main gate of the airport without any checks, and onto the main Mombasa road. The car traveled along the potholed tarmac for another nine hours. It was hot and dusty. The six members of the group were dozing or just staring out of the window as the African scenery passed by. At 19:00, just after nightfall, the group arrived in Malindi. Here they would spend the night in a local two-star hotel, so as to bring no unwanted attention. Malik checked the group in using the names from the passports, then instructed his men to go to their rooms and wash and pray. Going to a mosque was out of the question, too many prying eyes and these African's loved to chat. The driver was from Abdi. He did not talk during the journey, he just dropped them at the hotel and said he would return at 06:00 to collect them.

After praying they sat and chatted away the evening, then into the night. No one was tired after sitting all day long. They were fit soldiers and needed to get rid of the excess energy. The group of six men decided a walk around the town would be safe. The streets were quiet now the bustle of the day was long over. The roughly-paved, dark streets led them to the center of town. There was music coming from some local bars and cafés, with girls outside standing and talking or dancing in the street. In Palestine, you did not see the girls dressed like this. These young ladies were hardly covered. It was obscene, but the newcomers were only looking. The young soldiers drank Coke and water the whole night, sitting at the edge of the fun watching the girls. Occasionally one or two, then three, came over, chatting and dancing with them. The young, friendly girls sat down at the table and even on their laps, giggling and laughing, teasing these strong immature men. Everyone spoke fluent English as did Malik and his gang. It was all good fun. The girls offered much more than just chatting, but Malik told his guys no, this was not the time.

At midnight, they headed back to the hotel. Malik warned, "Guys, we need to be serious now. We are on a mission, so no messing around."

The others agreed and headed off towards their rooms. Malik was the first to have a sick feeling in his stomach. As he reached into his jacket for his key and felt nothing. The panic started rising in his throat, he checked all his pockets, cursing loudly in Arabic, "No! No! No!"

Then Joab came running, "Malik, I have lost my wallet, my keys, and my phone."

Malik looked up, he said, "Shit! Me the same."

Malik and Joab raced out into the road, running as fast as they could down the quiet, empty streets until they came to the center of town. The café was dark. They had been conned. The girls were playing them all along and must have been waiting for them to leave, then lock the doors immediately and make off with their take.

Malik ran back to the hotel and woke the others. He demanded, "Check your pockets. What have you lost?" Each member of the team sleepily checked their pockets.

The thieves had gotten away with three wallets and two mobile phones. This was serious. The team had used the phones for all sorts of information. Joab the bomb maker had lost his phone, and Malik had as well along with his wallet.

He took another phone off one of the others. Malik was grateful for making the group divide their money up for their trip between themselves. The thieves had successfully taken half of it. They would have to be careful from now on.

He felt guilty he had allowed these half-naked, wanton women to twist his brain and stop him thinking. The group had failed before they had begun. He had to do better than this. No more mistakes, or his father would have his head.

The Toyota Landcruiser picked the group at 06:00 exactly. The driver sat outside hooting the horn as if he was not happy about his duties. Malik and his team gratefully trouped out to the waiting vehicle with very low spirits. This leg of the journey was the same as yesterday, silence in the car as they sat contemplating their fate. Maybe the team had not been trained well enough. To be beaten before you begin by such a simple trick was so embarrassing to Malik. He would die of shame if his father ever found out. The road trip took another four hours of endless scrub and pothole-filled roads. Finally, the car turned off the tarmac, heading into the bush. After another twenty minutes of driving along rough tracks, they reached some large black gates. Malik was telling himself the incident in Malindi would never be found out, the phones would be wiped and sold locally to some street vendors. The Toyota drove through the gate, then up to some ornately carved wooden doors. A young, tall, thin man wearing a Kanzu was waiting for them. As soon as the group got out of the car, the driver drove off. The tall boy now took over. He did not greet them, just led them, without a word, through the large house to some rooms at the back. He pointed out the showers and latrines, then left them alone.

After a few minutes, a wail filled the compound. The cleric was calling them. The young soldiers of Allah automatically trooped out as one across the clearing. The young men removed their shoes and socks, washed their feet, hands and face, then filed into the mosque for prayer and forgiveness. The failure still hung over them. Malik knew they would not all be returning to Palestine. Some would die here. That was the plan. The lucky ones would be martyrs to the cause going straight to Paradise and finding their 'Houri', seventy-two virgins, all with large breasts and childbearing hips waiting for them, a gift from Allah himself for their devotion to the Muslim way of life.

Chapter Five

Wanjiku was sat in her bedroom behind the bar. As the only daughter and ten years older than Sunshine, she had been awarded her own room. The place was typical for Mtwappa: twelve feet square, a stout wooden door with a solid sliding bolt, and a rectangular window set into the outside wall, covered with a metal grill for safety. The floor and walls were bare, gray concrete. In the corner was a small sink for washing. Wanjiku had spent the last year trying to make it more of a home, collecting things she found around Mtwappa or was given by customers. The tourists always seemed to have flags of their own country. Often when it was time to leave, they would give them to Mwangi for his bar. She had pilfered them and put them on the walls. Hung in front of her was the American flag, then on the wall beside her the German, and on the other side a British one. The floor had several mats and odd bits of furniture she had come across. Right now, laying on her bed, she was gazing at the American Stars and Stripes. It had been given to her by an American boy who had come to do some missionary work further north in Kilifi District. She had been to Kilifi. It was a dry, dusty place; the roads went on forever. These young Americans had come to help build a church and an orphanage in the bush. On the way back, they had stopped in Mtwappa for a break before heading home.

The young, blond Christian had seen Wanjiku and fallen in love with her instantly. He had begged her to leave her family and travel with him to the USA. Wanjiku had felt excited. A real first world country just like the movies. Her mom and aunt had said, "You go, Wanjiku, it will be a beginning for us. You can send us money then we will come and join you."

The adventure had been great. The young boy, Martin, had sorted all the papers out for her to leave, sending money for her to go to school so her visa would be accepted. He had written to her for months and months. Then the much-awaited day had come. The appointment at the American Embassy. She had taken a 'Matatu,' the fourteen-seater mini busses that are everywhere on the African Continent, to Mombasa and the overnight bus to Nairobi.

She arrived in Nairobi the following morning. Getting off the bus, after twelve hours of traveling, weary and hot, her cousin was waiting at the busy terminal. HE took her directly to the American Embassy. She stood in the queue for nearly three hours, slowly trudging forward one step every twenty minutes, damp, sweaty, papers in her hand. She clearly remembered like it was yesterday. The light-skinned girl peering over the counter at her. "So, Ms Maria, you want to go to America."

Wanjiku had replied in her best English with an American twang. "Yes, it is the country of my dreams. My fiancé Martin has invited me."

The pale, young, disinterested girl sighed. "How long have you known your fiancé?" She said sarcastically.

Wanjiku thought for a second, "Well, six months. We have been writing every week. Look I have the letters."

The letters were waved off as unimportant. The immigration lady said impatiently. "How long in Kenya did you know your fiancé?"

Wanjiku replied, "Four weeks before he had to go back on the plane." Wanjiku could see in the cold gray eyes of this pale girl that her dream was slipping away.

The girl smirked, "Only four weeks and you are his fiancé!"

Wanjiku was getting annoyed now. She was tired from the journey and waiting so long. "Yes," she said. "Just because you are not so pretty and a man would not look at you does not mean a man would not fall for me in two hours!"

The interview had gone downhill very quickly from there. The pale, skinny girl had taken a few more details then confirmed the P.O. box and Martin's address. Wanjiku was sent back out into the sunlight. She knew there was no chance her application would be accepted. The skinny girl would not allow that. After miserably wandering around Nairobi for a couple of hours, she returned to the bus station, catching the bus back home to Mtwappa. Her family were disappointed. Martin's letters became less frequent, finally stopping altogether after a couple of months, he had probably found a skinny, American girl with pale gray eyes. It did not bother her too much, the family carried on as always hoping things would change making their way day to day.

Wanjiku was playing with the shiny new phone Brody had left with her. He was a good man, but she knew there would be no promises from him. He was wild and untamed, not like her Christian boy. Brody would be long gone very soon. But he was happy and great company, with a pocket full of cash, so what the hell, have some fun!

She flipped the phone open and pressed the green button with some strange black marks on it. The phone lit up, then started its process of finding the network and setting itself up. Once the machine was ready, it sat looking at her. The screen had some small pictures of things on it. She idly pressed the buttons on the main handset, looking and trying to read the menus for setting the time, making alarms, calling special people, etc. But it was impossible. The writing was just in strange wiggling lines.

When she hit the button for the envelope, a long list appeared, with names running down the side. She clicked the up and down arrows watching as the list moved one step at a time in the direction of the arrows. She pressed another button and the menu and list disappeared. After a few frustrating minutes of randomly pushing buttons, she managed to find the envelope again.

Scrolling up and down the list, she could see names of people, then if one name was highlighted she could click another button and a message would appear. But she could not understand the message as it was written in Arabic, like the letters plastering the outside of the mosque.

Wanjiku got bored, put the phone away, and left the room, heading out to Mtwappa to see what she could find today.

As usual, since before dawn, Brody had been up. The day in Africa always started early. Hassan would go and pray at around 04:00, returning to make the coffee and some African pastries or chapatti for breakfast, which was often followed by a Mango or some bananas. It was a very healthy way to live.

After a short break, Brody headed off on his morning ritual run. Racing to the tree and back, he was feeling stronger every day. Running on the sand was tough. It made his legs burn as the sand was soft and his feet would dig in, not like running on the road where you bounced to the next step. The sand dragged his feet down. It was like running up a hill with a fifty-pound pack on your back. His legs were on fire after the first two and a half miles. Then his lungs could not get enough oxygen from the short gasps he was forced to make. But he would charge on and on until he had mastered the distance. Once back at *Shukran*, he would dive straight over the side and swim to the middle of the creek and back again.

Brody sat at the back of *Shukran*, recovering from the morning torture," Gumbao, where are you? Are you onboard?"

Brody could hear Gumbao's muffled shouts, "Down here, boss."

He lifted the engine hatch, "What you doing, Gumbao?"

Gumbao smiled his toothless smile. "Just checking, boss. She is a lovely engine, we need to keep her going. She is old, but gold."

Gumbao loved the engine. It was a four-cylinder Yanmar from South America, about 120 hp. But they were not sure, as all the engine marks and numbers had been carefully removed many years ago. Since Hassan was the cook and general dog's body, Gumbao decided he would be the head engineer and had taken on the work of looking after the Yanmar. It was now spotless and running smoothly. The wooden engine room was decorated with the tools Brody had bought. Oils and fluids were carefully placed in another section created between some ribs.

Gumbao had taken to sleeping in the engine room. His bedroll was stored in the corner out the way. Brody was amazed at how he had just decided he was now the engineer, disappearing one day and coming back with tools and advice on what to do. Brody was no mechanic, he was a soldier. He could make things work or blow them up. Fiddling with engines was not his idea of fun. But Gumbao had become a fundi of sorts, over the last few weeks. When something went wrong, he disappeared and came back either with a friend or the answer to the problem.

Africa was a strange place full of odd ways and systems. People just lived. If things changed they changed. When circumstance altered which meant you had to do change your behavior, there was never a complaint. Everyone just got up and got on with it. A few months ago, Gumbao had been living in Pemba using a dhow and fishing. Now he was in Mtwappa, living on Brody's dhow and was the engineer. Gumbao didn't even have a change of clothes. When Brody gave him money he just went and got drunk. His life was simple. Brody supplied the food as part of his wages. He only needed one pair of shorts and a shirt. He did not own a pair of shoes he had never seen the need for them.

Gumbao was showing Brody how he had tightened the belts on the flywheel to the alternator with his new spanners when they heard a shout from the jetty.

"Hi Brody, it's me Wanjiku," Brody looked out at her. She was in very tight blue jeans with a bright yellow shirt with 'PRADA' proudly stretched across her breasts in black. Her hair had changed again. It was now long, past her shoulders.

Brody smiled. "Hi, what you doing? You come to visit us?"

Wanjiku replied. "For sure, Captain. How do I get on this thing?"

Brody walked to the gunwale and laid out the gangplank. Wanjiku danced along the short, narrow piece of wood onto the deck. Brody offered her a cold Tusker. When they had opened them and sat in the stern cabin in the shade Wanjiku said, "These phones are rubbish."

Brody asked, "Why?"

Wanjiku went on, "Look, the writing is all wrong. It looks like the mad scribbles of the Koran."

Brody had not even looked at his phone, so took Wanjiku's to see, "Shit," he said, "They must have been set up for the Middle East. This is Arabic. I bet there is a switch to turn them back to English."

Wanjiku said, "You think it's just a switch or a setting? There are loads of things you can do, but I can't read it. Not even the numbers are right."

She showed Brody the envelope sign on the screen of the phone, pressing the buttons, scrolling through the list of different names. When she finally managed to open one of the messages, it was all in Arabic, so they could not understand what it meant.

Wanjiku said, "I have a friend called Amir. He is clever and knows all about radios, and T. V.'s. He even fixed Dad's fridge, maybe he will know the right button to click."

Brody was happy for the chance of an excursion, "Cool, let's go find him."

They walked through the bar to the car park, Wanjiku called a PikiPiki over for a ride to town. The seat was designed for two Chinese people. Now it would have to suffer two Africans and a 'Muzungu.' There was not much room. Brody had to sit right up close to Wanjiku, the closest he had ever been. She smelled good. Looking over her shoulder, smiling that huge white-toothed smile she said. "You better hold onto my waist or you'll fall off."

Brody held on all the way to town enjoying the feel of her firm, muscular body.

The small shop at the end of the dingy street was more of an open-air market stall than an actual electronics store. The front door flipped up. Amir was sat almost in the street with his stock spread out behind him. He could touch the back wall easily. The place was packed with radios, televisions, DVD players and there were two fridges on the path in front of him. Above, he had flashing Christmas lights with a For Sale sign.

Amir took the phone and looked at it, he glanced up at Brody then at Wanjiku. "You will have to leave it with me. It will take some time, about an hour or two. Come back at 3 pm."

As soon as they were out of site, Amir, closed his shop, leaving in the opposite direction, heading into the small houses behind the main road. He zig-zagged around the houses, turning left and right through the tight, narrow, dirty streets of Mtwappa. He constantly checked behind to see if anyone was following. The circuitous, cautious route led him to the narrow alley next to the mosque. He removed his shoes and quickly entered.

The cleric, Bashar, was inside preparing for the afternoon prayer when Amir found him. He quickly showed him the phone and the messages. Bashar went into his office at the rear of the mosque and dialed a number he knew by heart.

A quiet voice picked up on the second ring. "Salaam Alekum."

He replied. "Alekum Salaam."

"Bashir, my friend, you are calling me, why?" The voice requested.

"Mzee, I have a piece of equipment here, I think it belongs to you," Bashir replied.

The old man sat up in his chair in Kikambala. "What could you possibly have that I would want, Bashir?"

The cleric said. "A new telephone has been handed to me. There is writing in Arabic on the screen. I can see it has been used in Palestine from the numbers. I was told you have some guests."

Abdi thought for a second, then spoke, "I am coming to the mosque now. Wait for me there."

Abdi put down the phone and called the tall, thin Somali boy to get his car ready immediately.

Brody and Wanjiku were sitting in her father's bar enjoying some Nyama Choma, a grilled beef delicacy. Wanjiku, a member of the Kikuyu Tribe was an expert at roasting meat. She had been brought up on a staple diet of the stuff. Brody had sat in the bar enjoying a drink while Wanjiku had talked to the cook and asked for the choicest cuts of beef for the day. There was always a large bottle of the special marinade in the fridge ready for these occasions.

Once they had lit the barbecue grill with charcoal and let it settle for a while, she had roasted the meat over the coals. The cook served Kachumbari, a local salad of onions, thinly sliced tomato, and chilies. This was accompanied with Ugali, a maize meal which is ground to a fine powder then mixed with boiling water until it becomes a solid block. The Ugali is broken off in pieces and eaten by hand.

The meal was going well, the beer was flowing, and they were having a good time. Mwangi had been in and out a few times, but was busy working on his other projects, as he called them.

The bar had been full over lunchtime. Wanjiku had served food and drinks for her father then sat at the bar with Brody, laughing and talking. No one had noticed the three medium-sized guys with lightweight jackets come in through the kitchen entrance and sit quietly by the door. There was nothing conspicuous about them. Just regular looking guys out for some lunch and a drink, but they held themselves well and were obviously fit. The three men sat quietly in the corner, drinking Coke, surveying the room expertly. When the leader was happy, he walked over to the bar. At the same time, one of the others casually wandered over to the television next to the door to the salon. The place was now effectively covered, all the exits were sealed. The head man could now conduct his questioning. If anyone made a bolt for it, firstly, they would know where to look for information, and before the person could leave he would be floored by one of his companions.

The head man at the bar asked casually. "Does anyone know where Mwangi is?"

Wanjiku, instantly wary, said, "Ah, he is out, for now, we do not know when he will come back. He just comes and goes."

Brody's ears pricked up. He could see the guy at the bar held himself well, and would probably be dangerous in a fight. It was odd to see someone wearing a jacket, even a lightweight one, in this heat.

The guy said, "Can't you call him? I need to speak to him urgently."

At the same time, he glanced over towards the door. Brody spotted the nod and noticed a similar guy at the door acknowledge the glance.

Wanjiku said, "Sorry but I have no way of contacting him. Sit and have a drink, maybe he will come back, or tell me your name and leave a message."

The guy smiled, "I'll sit and wait," As he spoke to Wanjiku, he glanced in the other direction. Brody was watching closely now. Another guy over by the television acknowledges the look.

At that moment, Mwangi walked into the half-full bar. He looked a bit worried, but he always looked a bit worried.

Wanjiku knew the routine. There were often people asking after Mwangi. A lot of his deals were on the edge of what was right and wrong. Some fell over the edge completely. She saw her father go into the kitchen. The guys saw him too, but apparently did not know what he looked like as they ignored him.

Wanjiku quietly left and found her dad, "What have you been up to?" Mwangi looked shocked as usual. "Nothing, girl, I'm fine. Don't worry about me." Wanjiku went on. "But Dad there is a guy at the bar asking for you."

Mwangi went to the serving hatch and cautiously peered through. Brody was sat at the bar with another stranger next to him.

The guy guarding the back door had noticed Wanjiku leave the bar. He followed her quietly down the corridor. The man at the bar noticed the guard had moved and signaled to his friend to go back to the door.

Brody was watching this unfold. He had to consider what to do. This could be innocent. They might be looking for a deal. But his gut told him this was not the case. These guys wanted Mr Mwangi for something, not to buy something from him. He leaned back so he could see the two guys. It was no good the angles were all wrong. Casually, he moved to a better point, mid-way between the men in the bar and able to see through the serving hatch. Mr

Mwangi and Wanjiku were talking. The third guy was moving along the corridor to their right, he was still hidden from their view in the passage.

It was time to consider his position. He could stop these two easily, but the third one could be a problem. He was creeping up on Wanjiku in the kitchen. There must be knives there, it could get ugly quickly.

As the third guy entered the kitchen, Mr Mwangi and Wanjiku stopped their discussion and looked at him. Mwangi said. "Can I help you, sir?"

The guy smiled and said, "I've come to pick you up Mwangi. We need to take you somewhere for a long chat. You took something from my boss and he wants it back."

Mwangi stepped back. Brody could see what was happening, but the two guys in the bar could not.

He inched a step closer to the back door, staggering slightly and cradling his beer. He was within striking distance now. Up close, the guy watching the back door seemed fit and strong, probably fast too. There was one difference between this team and Brody. This was what he had been trained for. He had done it so many times before it was second nature. The rooky by the door had been trained to fight, probably in a gym. He had no scars. A brawler always has scars. The easiest way know if you should walk away was to look at their hands, broken blood vessels and bruised knuckles the swelling never goes down. But more importantly, he had not been trained to keep a close eye on his surroundings, who was close-by, especially his blindside, where the attack always comes from.

The guy at the bar was not moving. He was the boss and was expecting to just do the talking and get out. But he did have a suspicious bulge on his left hip, maybe that was what the jacket was for.

The man in the kitchen was moving towards Mwangi and Wanjiku, slowly talking his way forward, step by step, until he was close enough to strike. Mwangi looked frightened. He was a dealer, not a fighter.

Wanjiku was staring at him with her dark brown eyes. If looks could kill, he would have been dead.

Brody saw the man in the kitchen reach out to grab Mwangi. It was a slow, self-assured movement. He was up against a frightened man and a girl, this was an easy takedown.

Mwangi backed off, but the man kept coming, pushing Wanjiku away and grabbing Mwangi's arm. Then Brody saw it in slow motion. Wanjiku picked a knife from the table as she was pushed away. The guy grabbed her father and as he did so, he put the other hand on the table to steady himself to drag her dad out of the room. Wanjiku's arm came around in a slow curve, Brody could not see the total arc of the curve, and he did not see the knife as it went through the guy's hand, pinning him to the table. But he did hear the immediate scream from the kitchen. The guy by the door was fast, but Brody was faster. He tripped him as he started to move, then simply grabbed his shoulders as he was falling and threw him against the door frame. The crown of his head hit the center of the solid frame with such force the wall shook, loosening plaster which fell in a white flurry onto the unconscious guy's back. Blood started oozing from the top of his head.

He turned to see the second guy moving straight through the crowd towards him. The crowd were reacting to the screaming in the kitchen, Brody was not. He watched the guy move. He was fast, but not trained to the level Brody was. Brody had been trained in close-quarter urban combat. In the special forces, he had cleared houses or buildings, every door you kick in or enter is potentially lethal. You are trained to do. Not think. Every threat has to be eliminated with total efficiency.

Brody let him come at him. He swung once, then a kick, then Brody punched him straight with knuckles slightly bent. His punch connected with the guy's larynx. The forward movement of the man and the forward movement from Brody connected at the guy's throat. He had been moving to get a blow to Brody's head a split second earlier. The attacker knew he was good and fast. This had never happened to him before. Within a split second, he had been stopped. Now his lungs were empty. And he could not breathe. Then the pain and the panic hit him. He stood and looked at Brody with his huge, bulging, panicked eyes. He did not know what to do. His legs buckled, Brody caught him and slid him into a chair. The guy just looked at Brody not believing what had happened.

As Brody relieved him of the Glock 17 strapped to his hip, he said, "Relax and breathe, just relax and breathe. It will pass. Then you go, and I never see you again. If I see or hear of you around here, I will find you and kill you." The guy just nodded.

Brody ran to the kitchen. Wanjiku was standing like she was paralyzed. Her father was staring at the wall. The man was screaming. Only about 9 seconds had passed from the blade being picked from the table to Brody entering the room. He grabbed the knife and yanked it out of the wooden table. The guy screamed again. Brody pulled him into the corridor. Blood was flowing out of the guy's hand all over the floor. As he moved, it sprayed on the walls. He dragged the wounded man along the short corridor then slammed him up against the door frame. The guy's partner was laying at their feet, bleeding from his head. Brody said exactly the same to this man, who nodded his agreement. He could not believe what had happened either. Brody pushed him roughly into the bar, throwing a cloth at him to wrap his hand.

When he got back to the kitchen, everyone seemed like they were waking up from a dream. Wanjiku realized what she had done and started to cry. She was not a violent person. Mwangi marshaled himself. And shouted, "Sunshine! Sunshine!" The boy appeared from the back rooms, "Go get Corporal Naivasha. Run! Run now, boy!" Sunshine ran off out through the door to find the policeman.

Brody asked, "Will you be OK? These guys were tough and well trained. They were not robbers or thugs."

Mwangi was still in shock he smiled, and said, "Thanks, my boy. You saved us. I am fine. When Corporal Naivasha arrives, he will lock these bastards up. Then I'll make sure every policeman in Mtwappa knows there is a hot plate of food here and a cold Tusker on the house. This place will be safer than the State House."

Brody nodded, then Mwangi went on, "But you and Wanjiku must leave. The police should not find you here, or they will ask questions. Wanjiku you go and stay with your Aunt. I will send Sunshine later and your mom." She just nodded showing her agreement. Wanjiku was still dealing with what had happened.

Brody took her hand and led her out of the bar, across the street to a PikiPiki. He put her on the seat, got on behind her, and told the driver to go to the Full Moon Bar.

When they got to the bar, Brody shouted, "Hassan. Hassan, come!" In a few minutes, Hassan came walking towards them, he was smiling his usual smile. "Boss, Jambo, how are you?" He said.

Brody said, "Go to *Shukran*, find my small rucksack, and bring it here as quickly as you can."

In a few minutes, Brody had the second phone in his hands. He flicked it open and turned it on. Then he figured out how to get the envelope to open and found the list of names. He opened one of the messages and handed it to Hassan.

Hassan had been brought up on the Koran, speaking Arabic before he could speak Swahili. All the Muslims on the island did the same. Every day when he was a child, he would go to madrassa where he would learn to chant the passages of the Koran over and over. As the words became familiar to the young boys, the clerics would tell them the meanings. As the young students grew, they would read passages from the Koran to the younger kids and make them chant it over and over.

Hassan looked at the writing for a few seconds, his mouth moving instinctively with the words, then he stopped. "Bwana, this is bad. The message is telling me how to make a bomb."

Brody just looked. "What!"

Hassan went on, "Yes, it is talking about putting wires together to make a connection so a timer will work. Then it says when the timer hits zero it will explode."

Brody took the phone and opened another message, "And this?" he asked.

Hassan took the phone, "Yes, this is similar. It is talking about a much bigger explosion. It talks of a car exploding when the button is pressed."

Brody did not know what to do. This was serious. His mind was racing through all the possibilities. Something was happening here he did not understand. One thing was certain, it was undoubtedly linked to those three guys that came into the bar and Amir's shop. He was going to have to work this out, then go and find this Amir and get some answers.

Chapter Six

Brody and Hassan went back to Mtwappa. Brody was deep in thought trying to figure out what exactly was happening. Why had the guys come to the bar to find Mwangi? They had said he had annoyed someone and had to go meet them. Mwangi had sworn he had not been doing anything unusual except the new phones business.

They wandered around the back alleys of Mtwappa until they were behind Amir's shop. They hid behind another stall watching the comings and goings without being seen. Hassan had been working on the boat so was not part of the group. He had been staying mostly at the marina and had not visited the town, especially not with Brody. No one would connect the two so he stayed in front. The tiny shop was open and busy, Amir carrying on his business as usual. Several people came and went as the time ticked by. Brody had sat and waited like this for days at a time when he was in the Navy, watching patiently until something breaks and he could move on.

After about an hour, a large man came walking in from the street. Hassan nudged Brody to look at the guy. Hassan said, "Boss, I know that guy. He's the cleric at the mosque." The cleric and Amir had a hushed conversation, Amir looked worried.

As soon as the Bashar left, Amir closed his shop and locked up for the day.

Brody and Hassan followed behind Amir as he wound his way through the narrow, dirty alleyways that made up the back streets of Mtwappa. People were selling and living on the street, beggars and pushbikes all trying to live in the squalor of an urban slum. They stepped over open drains, and kicked through roaming mongrel dogs, then rounding a corner following as far behind Amir as they dared. He suddenly cut down a narrow alley back to the main road. Brody broke into a jog so as not to lose their prey. He reached the top of the lane, which was just a gap of a couple of feet between two metal shacks, just in time to see Amir get to the end and cut to the left. Hassan joined him panting in his ear, "Where did he go, boss?"

Brody and Hassan crept along as fast as they could, dodging the puddles in the small path between the shacks. Hassan was ahead, as Amir would not know him if he looked and Brody had a better chance of staying hidden in the shadows.

When Hassan reached the end of the lane, he peered in the direction Amir had disappeared, just catching a glimpse of him as he washed his feet and entered the mosque. Hassan usually prayed on the boat as he did not know anyone in Mtwappa, but he could go into any mosque in the world and be welcomed.

Hassan whispered to Brody. "Boss, let me go in. They do not know me. Maybe I can listen and hear something to help us."

Brody nodded, "Hassan, be careful. Don't take any risks. We can get the information in many different ways, so just scout around and have a look."

"Ah, boss, if they are planning something bad, I do not want the name of Allah to be brought into disrepute. I will protect our savior with my life," he replied.

Brody was shocked this guy was not usually that brave, but when his religion was being affected he would risk life and limb to save it.

He nodded and Hassan wandered out into the sunlight and nonchalantly strolled over to the mosque, washed his hands and feet, then entered the dark shadows of the interior.

Brody moved back into the dark, dirty alley and waited for his friend to return. The years of missions and training had left him with a sixth sense. He knew when his gut started feeling the way it did right now, things were not going well. He needed to think of a plan and people who could help. This felt bigger than him, not something he could just do on his own.

Hassan walked into the building. All mosques, however large or small, are basically the same in design. The only real difference is size and grandeur, Mtwappa mosque was a small-town affair without any of the fancy trappings of the city mosques. Even Hassan's mosque back in Pemba was more ornate that his one. It was for functional prayer, for busy people trying to adhere to the ways of Allah and also make a living in a busy, growing town.

He moved around the outside of the large square praying area. He was not here to pray today. There were a couple of people kneeling at the front, chanting quietly from the Koran. Hassan understood the prayers but had no desire to join in today. Usually, he would have gone and knelt next to one of the people and joined in with them to make them feel better.

On one side of the praying square, he noticed a small corridor leading towards the back. There was no one around, so he wandered along and down the passageway, making sure he did not make a sound on the polished, bare, concrete floor.

At the end of the corridor was an office. The door was ajar. Hassan slipped across the smooth concrete, making no noise. Positioning himself to the left of the opening, he listened to the conversation coming from inside.

Bashir was talking in quiet tones to Amir. "Brother, the attack did not go as planned. There was a 'Muzungu' as you said, but he beat Abdi's men like they were children."

Amir replied as he wrung his hands in despair, "That is not good. What am I to do? They will guess I have told you of the phone. I am sure they will come. If this 'Muzungu' is like you say, he will kill me."

Bashir said, "Yes, I think he will. He frightens me too. I am a peaceful man. I do not fight like these uncivilized Europeans."

Amir asked, "What shall I do, must I hide?"

Bashir replied, "Yes. Go to Abdi in the bush at Kikambala. He has said you can sleep there until this is over. It will not be not long, and Allah will provide for us all."

Amir said, "But what about my shop, my business?"

Bashir looked at him. "This is the fight against the infidels, my brother. Business does not even matter at this time. Go to Abdi and pray, you will be safe there."

Amir nodded. He knew he could not stay in Mtwappa now, it was too dangerous. He had to leave for a while. He would disappear, his wife and children would have to wait patiently for his return.

Outside in the corridor, Hassan sensed the conversation was ending, suddenly realizing he was trapped in a dead-end. Amir could come out at any moment. He looked around in a panic, getting caught or even seen here would be a death sentence after what he had just heard. He saw a mop and a bucket in the corner. Grabbing it, he started mopping the floor quietly. After a couple of seconds, he slopped some water on the floor with a loud slap so the occupants of the room would hear him.

Amir came out of the room and looked at the small scruffy man mopping the floor. He nodded at him curtly, as was the custom with household staff, and walked away. Hassan smiled. No one ever sees the person sweeping the floor, they are invisible.

He hurried out of the mosque as soon as he saw Amir disappear around the corner at the end of the passageway.

Brody watched Amir leave the mosque. The man did not look left or right, but hurried directly to the street and got onto one of the local busses they called 'Matatus,' heading north.

A few seconds later, Hassan appeared and ducked back into the narrow, stinking alleyway.

"Boss, this is bad. I heard them talking. Amir is going to stay with Abdi in Kikambala, that's where you went with Barry the other day."

"What did you hear?" Brody asked.

"They know about you, and say you are too tough for them. The cleric sent Amir to Abdi's house at the beach. He said it will all be over soon and not to go back to his shop." Hassan continued, "Boss, it is not safe for you here, they are going to do something I know. If you are in the way, they will get rid of you."

Brody had already decided this was way above his pay scale. He wracked his brain searching for suitable answers. No one would listen with the current level of intel. It would be hard to be taken seriously at the best of times. He had only scant information and gut feelings nothing amounting to real proof, he had to find something more concrete to escalate this to a higher level. The only next step was to get more information, enough to convince someone in authority there was something here to look at. Everything led to Abdi's house in Kikambala. That was the obvious first choice for any kind of surveillance.

There were hire and rental shops all along the main street for tourists to rent scooters or big muscle bikes to show off to the local girls. After ten minutes, Brody was set with a Honda RD200 off-road trail bike. This bike was designed for severe off-road usage, exactly what was needed for this task. He told Hassan to go back to the boat and explain everything to Gumbao, then wait for him to return. Brody knew Gumbao could handle himself if needed and would look after Hassan.

The lightweight Honda HR 200 was designed for this kind of work, powerful with a lot of torque low down, ideal for driving through deep sand. The tires were designed with large lumpy-treads ideal for work in soft mud, but not so good on the road. Brody jumped on the bike, kick-started it, then clicked up with his left toe, putting it into first gear. He slowly let the clutch lever out with his right until the engine started to bite. He pulled out onto the main drag, weaving in and out of the maelstrom of the traffic. It was like a blizzard with vehicles for snowflakes coming at you from all directions at once. Malindi Road, as it was known, was busy. At just past twelve, everyone had somewhere to go. The rules were very simple, there were none. It was a mad free for all. Just get where you want to go, giving way was a sign of weakness!

The Matatus, fourteen seater minibuses painted in garish colors with music blaring from the windows, would swerve either out from the curb to get back onto the road, or into the curb after overtaking to drop or pick a passenger. There were no bus stops or laybys. The road and the curb were the same and free for parking, driving, or waiting. The minibuses were noisy and full, way more than 14 people, more like twenty. With no room left for the conductor, he slid the door back and swung out of the vehicle holding precariously onto the roof rack where the belongings of the passengers were stacked. This, combined with the PikiPikis the bicycles and the human traffic, made it a dangerous drive until Brody broke out from the main drag and headed north towards Kikambala.

Once on the open road, he could open the small 200HP engine up, covering the distance almost as quickly as the Landrover.

He went straight past the junction Barry had taken a few days before, continuing for about a kilometer then making a sharp right along an unused, overgrown track. The bike was light but had gutsy low gearing, it could power through the sand and dirt, flying over the ruts in the track. The off-road tires bit into the sand and soil, pulling the bike and rider along at about 60 mph.

Brody decided to head across country towards the compound. His plan was to approach it from the north. When they had visited the other day, the main gate was the only entrance for traffic, reducing the need for more guards. The place was quiet and out of the way. Abdi was an arrogant old man, feeling safe in the bush. There would probably be four guards maybe less. He continued racing on through the scrub, weaving in and out of the thorned Acacia trees, following the goat tracks, across the flat, barren, burnt wasteland towards the coast. Soon Brody could see tall coconut trees in the distance. These would provide him with cover to approach Abdi's compound. The sun was directly overhead. Even though he was traveling fast the heat was still burning his back and face. The dust was continuous, billowing around the bike. He raced on across the Savannah, heading east until the Indian Ocean appeared, glistening in the distance. Then turned south towards Abdi's house.

After another twenty minutes of driving between the palms, the large compound became visible through the trees. Stopping the bike and shutting off the noisy engine, Brody left it hidden in the undergrowth, then walked slowly and quietly through the bush towards the high, white walls. As he got closer, he could see the walls had been built either to keep someone out or in. They were easily twelve feet high and the flat tops had broken bottles embedded in the sloping surface. Above the glass was razor wire. At each corner was a floodlight. The silver metallic units looked old and a bit rusty, probably complacency. If nothing went wrong, why bother with maintenance? A good sign.

Keeping about thirty feet from the walls in the cover of the bush, he dodged along the northern side of the building, looking for a suitable point to enter the compound. The high-security wall made it almost impossible to do a straight climb and jump. He would be spotted immediately. Slowly making his way east, he soon heard the waves breaking on the shore. A few minutes later, the golden, sandy beach appeared. The wall continued for about another fifteen feet, then turned south, continuing at the same height. Brody felt exposed as he slowly made his way along the beachside of the compound. There was no obvious security, no guards or cameras. This was strange, perhaps Abdi felt so secure that they did not need any systems in place.

Brody came to a large metal gate in the eastern wall. He figured it must be about halfway along. The next corner where the wall turned back west was clearly visible just ahead. The gate was made from thick steel, painted black with a sturdy, reinforced frame set into the wall. It had been built very well, fitting perfectly on all sides. The bottom had some sort of hard rubber flap, it was impossible to get a glimpse inside. Behind him, running out to the reef line some four hundred feet away, was a channel cut into the limestone, effectively making a deep-water inlet right into the compound. Someone had gone to a lot of trouble and expense to do this. Brody wondered why someone would invest so much to make a slipway with deep water access in this out of the way place.

The reef at this point was sporadic and broken. As Brody looked out towards the ocean, he could see there were many inlets through the rocks. A mid-sized, shallow draft boat with a knowledgeable captain could easily drive through, coming right up to the door of the compound.

Brody continued to the corner, turning west. He had to be extra vigilant. This was the side with the large gate they had pulled up to in the Loner a few days ago. It was, therefore, the busy side; more people, deliveries general comings and goings. Maybe a guard or two wandering around, keeping an eye on things, earning their pay. He surveyed the length of the compound but came up empty. There was nowhere to get easy access to the inside of the place. Particularly as it was broad daylight, an attempt at scaling the wall would be foolish, to say the least, he would be seen in an instant. Hiding in the bush a short way along the overgrown track, he watched the gate for an hour. A couple of cars came and went but nothing unusual. The place looked dead. It was silent.

After retracing his steps to the beach then back into the bush he arrived at his starting point. Brody found the bike in the bush where he had left it and decided to return after nightfall to make a proper ingress and see what was going on.

After leaving the Honda in town then catching a Piki Piki back to the boat, Brody immediately started preparing for the night sortie.

He called Hassan, "Tonight, we will go out, back up north. I will be doing a night dive inshore just off the reef. What are the tides like?"

Hassan thought for a second, "Boss. It's not brilliant, but OK. The tides are on neaps, not much movement so low currents. The high tide is around 'Saa tano usiku'. Shit, sorry boss. Around 23:00."

Brody thought for a minute, planning the evening, "Cool, that serves my purpose. How long will it take to get to Kikambala?"

Gumbao answered, "If we motor in about three hours, the current will be pushing north and with the neaps, the water will be calm."

Brody said, "Brilliant. Make sure the dive tanks are full and we have enough fuel for a return journey."

With that, he wandered off to the bar.

Around 20:00, they untied *Shukran* from the stone jetty, started the engines, and edged out into the creek. Brody set the radar, depth sounder and GPS on the Lowrance HDS10, splitting the screen into two, the radar overlay over the GPS. Now they could monitor their relative position and have the dark red radar overlay showing them obstructions. The wooden dhow slipped through the water with only the faint hum of the Yanmar. In total darkness, almost invisible.

Brody asked Hassan, "The moon tonight, Hassan. What will we see?"

Hassan grinned back, "Bwana Brody, it is no moon tonight, we are on our own. There will be no light on the ocean."

That suited the purpose. *Shukran* could sit just offshore in the darkness.

They motored out of the creek, turning north as soon as *Shukran* was clear of the breakers. Their journey was twelve miles along the coast. It would take about three hours. The crew took their stations, keeping four miles offshore in the darkness, watching the instruments the whole way. The water washed against the bow as the dhow cruised along at a steady six knots. Brody looked as the stars started to come out. This place was fantastic at night. He could see why the Muslims used the night more than the day. They could navigate, tell the time, know where they were all in the cycle of the moon.

As the stars pricked into life one by one, Brody realized he could see so many more than on land. The light pollution in the ocean is virtually zero. The boat was at least three miles offshore. No other ships were in sight. All around them was pitch black.

He was witness to a magnificent view of the Milky Way, which seemed so close you could almost reach out and touch it.

They passed the Peponi Hotel where there were some twinkling lights on the shoreline. The guests were probably enjoying the warm tropical evening, having dinner on the beach. After about an hour and a half, Gumbao started edging them back towards the mainland. Brody knew roughly the location on the coast in relation to the other hotels.

But Hassan with his keen eyes would be the one to tell them exactly where to slow and then stop, holding position just off the breakers. After about another forty minutes of slowly motoring along the coast, Hassan pointed out the break in the reef and then the long white wall on the beach. They were about fifty yards off the reef line. The small break between the broken reef and the beach was another three hundred yards north. Hassan pointed out the entrance the boats would use to head directly for the cut channel to the gate.

Brody laid out the plan to Gumbao and Hassan, "I will go in just about here. Head through the reef and up the channel. Once I am on-site, I will go over the wall and check out the inside. Give me an hour and a half, tops. If you hear any shouting or shooting head out to sea. Return in an hour to this spot, do the same three times. If you don't find me, head back to the creek."

Gumbao and Hassan nodded their agreement and set about preparing the dive equipment. Brody went below and opened the seaman's bag, taking out the Glock he had taken from the thug at the bar, checking the magazine, then put the gun in a waterproof bag.

Back on deck, his equipment was ready. He had one aluminum air cylinder set at 3000psi. This was plenty of air. It was a shallow dive, he would stay at less than thirty feet below the surface the whole way. Hassan helped him into the BCD, Buoyancy Control Device, then he slipped on the Suunto dive watch, with built-in compass. Once he was comfortable and had made sure the air was on. The standard check for air was to take several deep breaths through the regulator. At the same time look at the pressure gauge, if the needle did not move everything was OK. If it moved, he would have taken the air from the pipe between the first stage on his tank and the second stage, in his mouth. The needle on the gauge would drop to zero, a really bad thing underwater!

Then he put on his mask and fins, made sure his dive knife was attached to his calf, and checked that the spare was in the pocket of the BCD. With his fins on, he stepped off the ocean side of *Shukran* so the splash could not be seen or heard from the beach. Surfacing, he signaled to Gumbao that he was OK, deflated the jacket, turned on the small underwater torch and submerged.

As soon as he was below the surface, everything changed. All he could hear were his bubbles and the deep inhales as the air was sucked from the tank through the two valves into his lungs. Slowly descending into the darkness, Brody could remember his dive instructor. "Slow, long, steady breaths, never panic, keep cool and always breathe."

His dive computer was glowing on his arm showing the depth slowly increase. When it hit thirty feet Brody blew some air into the jacket to create neutral buoyancy. He was suspended in the dark, below was a thick void of blackness, above just visible silhouetted against the starlight was the line of *Shukran*'s hull. Brody looked around with his torch. There was nothing, he was all alone in the warm waters. His tight wetsuit clung to his body. It had taken in a thin layer of water when he had entered the ocean. As the water warmed from his body heat, it would return the favor and keep him warm by staying next to his skin.

He switched the Suunto dive computer to compass. The yellow glow of the swiveling L.E.D dial showing north, south, east, and west with a degree of heading in a small rectangular box at the bottom of the screen. Before stepping off *Shukran*, he had taken a bearing on the entrance to the channel of 272° W. He swam with the compass held firmly in front of his mask, just as he had been trained in the S.B.S. He held the torch to guide the way, following the bearing as best as he could. Dive training had been grueling. Navigation underwater is very difficult. There are no landmarks like hills or valleys to follow. You cannot feel your feet on the ground, so have no idea of speed or actual direction. Although he was swimming on a bearing, there was also the invisible current to consider, slowly pushing him north. He had gotten lost so many times in his early Navy days, coming up in completely the wrong place. It was only after hours and hours of long, cold nights swimming in rivers, lakes and oceans he had become competent enough to arrive at his destination. Brody felt disorientated and unsure of his position. But experience of well over two thousand dives taught him to keep going and keep his eyes open. *"Orienteering on land is a dream compared to a one hundred and fifty-yard swim at thirty feet in pitch-black waters,"* he thought to himself.

Brody finally came up to the start of the reef. He could see the ghost-like images of the night reef fish out hunting. The white-tipped reef sharks were moving around the reef looking for food. He slowly swam along over the top of the rocky outcrop. The place was still full of life. The nocturnal creatures were out. Crabs slide sideways around the sandy bottom until a grouper or white tip would swoop in and catch them with one swallow. Passing over a small crevice with what looked like a spider's web covering the entrance, a thick, impenetrable web of silk, he shone his light into the hole to see the sleeping parrotfish, safe in its cave for the night.

Brody knew the current was still from south to north. Although he did not know exactly where he had reached the coral, he figured he was probably pushed a bit north so decided to edge along the reef against the current. After swimming for about fifteen minutes. The water was getting shallower he was hugging the bottom just off the sand. Swinging the torch in a long, slow arc, hoping to see the entrance before he swam right passed it.

The beam only penetrated about ten feet into the inky blackness around him.

First, there was some debris, then more rocks on the bottom. Abdi's crew had blown the reef with dynamite. The reef along this coast is protected so he must have some friends in high places to get away with that! Brody swam into the entrance. The walls were rough the channel was wider than the distance the beam from the torch could penetrate. He swam along the bottom with his nose only a few inches off the stone floor, slowly finning along the channel. The water became shallower and shallower as he crossed the beach.

The computer on his arm sounded off when the depth was six feet. Slowly moving to the side of the channel for maximum cover, then holding his breath, he carefully rose to the surface, only his head silently appearing like a crocodile in a river, looking for prey. He removed the regulator then checked his surroundings. He was about forty feet short of the gate. There were no lights on the wall, everywhere was in darkness and silent. These guys were really confident. He stayed there for a whole ten minutes, holding the side of the channel as the waves slowly brushed against him, checking for any signs of life.

When he was completely satisfied it was quiet, he removed his BCD and weight belt and found a crevice in the rocks just below the surface pushing his equipment in. There was a flash as a huge octopus swam out of the hole. It looked at him with large angry eyes as it clumsily gathered its legs then sped off into the darkness. Brody rose breaking the surface and took a breath of fresh air, then sank back into the dark waters, silently swimming the short distance to the shore. He had the Glock and torch in his hand. His plan was to climb the gate, get inside, and look around. At night, he figured, it would be fine since the compound was dark. Someone clambering over the wall would not be seen. He had asked Hassan about dogs and been told Muslims don't like dogs so they probably would not have them around as guards.

Brody climbed the left side hinge of the gate and looked over the top. There were no obvious signs of guards patrolling. The gate had narrow spikes of steel pointing up from the framework, but the spaces between were just large enough for his feet. He was about sixty feet from the main house and the mosque, it was 23:00, the place was silent. A couple of windows in the house had streams of light, but there were no people or sounds. Looking around cautiously, he could see no sign of dogs. The animals keen senses would have heard him by now and come to investigate. He went silently over the gate, landing nimbly on the dry grass. To his left was an old wooden rowing boat that had been left upside down in the bushes. Someone had probably thought to come back and repair it, then make a living off the fish. But that was long ago, it sat forlornly with holes rotting through its hull, long forgotten. Brody gauged the sixty feet to the building. He figured there was no cover anyway, so the only option was to risk it and hope for the best. His wetsuit was black, only his face and hands would show up if a light was turned on. He took a deep breath and sprinted across the broken ground to the darkest corner of the house. There was silence, no dogs barking, no alarms being raised. So far so good.

He edged along the walls, quietly listening for any sound, moving swiftly, not wanting to be around the house too long. The longer he stayed, the more chance there was of him being found out. Without backup, he would be totally screwed. He found the back door and the long strip of windows: the accommodation block he had seen when they had visited a few days before. Brody moved silently, peering into the gloom of the first window. A young man was sleeping on the bed, the second was the same and the third. The fourth one was lit. Creeping below the window then adjusting himself to the far edge. He glanced in. There was a young, serious-looking guy sat at a desk, intently studying papers. The guy was frowning and mumbling to himself. Brody listened carefully but could not hear what he was saying.

Just as Brody was moving towards the next window, a door opened and shut. He stopped in his tracks and looked around. Off to one side next to a low wall were darker shadows, he darted towards them disappearing into the gloom. He took several deep breaths to keep calm and waited a few moments, then as he was trained, he waited for a few more moments, just to be sure. He was considering his next move when a side door opened. A medium-sized man exited and headed purposefully across the scrubby lawn. The guy knew where he was going, walking with a self-assured step in the darkness, striding across the open area, heading towards a small block built building near the wall. It looked like an outside toilet.

Brody was right. The guy quickly opened the door and went in, then a light clicked on. He silently crept across the open ground, feeling very exposed with the lights behind him. The latrine was about thirty-five feet from the main house. This would have to do. He needed information. It was much better for the information to come to him, rather than having to go look for it.

Brody waited patiently to the side of the toilet. After several minutes, the door started rattling. He stood right next to it on the hinge side. The door opened and the guy stepped out. As the door closed, Brody was standing in its place. The guy did not even see him in the darkness. His arm raised came down hard and fast, a straight hand chop to the vagus nerve in his neck. It would only stun the unsuspecting man for a couple of seconds, but that was enough for what was required. He used the time to clamp the guy's mouth shut and drag him further behind the hut into the darkness, holding his knife to the guy's throat for effect. The dive knife was large and heavy with a very polished blade, and it no doubt scared the shit out of the poor man. He was healthy and strong but not battle-hardened like Brody.

The guy just looked into Brody's eyes with terror. Brody motioned for him not to shout or scream, or he would slit his throat. The captured man nodded with staring eyes. Brody released his hold over the guy's mouth and whispered, "No shouting or yelling or you're dead. Do you understand English?"

The man nodded.

Brody said, "What's your name?"

The guy whispered, "Parvez."

Brody continued, "So, Parvez, where are you from, and why are you here?"

Parvez said, "Sir, I cannot tell you, or they will kill me." He pointed to the house.

Brody grinned, "Maybe they will kill you, maybe they won't. But right now, I've the knife to your throat, and I most certainly will kill you. Then I'll throw you down that old long drop toilet you were sat on. Those holes go down sixty or seventy feet, then twenty feet of pure shit. Your body won't be found for weeks, if ever, no one looks in the shitter for a dead body. Too much like hard work"

Parvez cringed at the thought, "But sir, I am only a follower. I do what I am told and nothing else."

"So, what are you told?" Brody asked.

"I am from Palestine. We arrived three days ago, me and five other boys. The leader is Malik. He is very strong and his father is very important. They trained us in the desert for our mission." Parvez blurted out in a hardly controlled whisper.

Brody pushed the knife against his throat until a thin line of red appeared. Parvez felt his skin being slit and continued quickly, "Honestly. I have no idea, it's all a secret. We arrived as I said. And were driven here after we stopped in a town further north." Parvez was keen to get the information out. He was sure this madman would kill him.

Brody asked, "I need more information. Tell me everything and quickly."

Parvez went on shakily, "We were trained in guns and explosives. The team is to make a raid on something, but I do not know what. We are from the Liberation Army of Palestine. I do not even know why I am here. There are no Jews here to kill."

Brody could not understand. He could see Parvez's point. Why come here they had enough trouble in their own country?

Brody said, "What about your host, what has he said to you?"

Parvez said, "He was furious. We stopped in a small town up north on the way here. We went out for some tea and sodas, then met some girls. They sat on our laps. We have never seen such behavior it was wicked, but we were weak. These ladies had hardly any clothes on, you could see their legs and arms, almost everything. We were weak, and Allah punished us. The girls stole our phones and our money. Mr Abdi found out about it, he has been shouting at us all night. We are ashamed and have to prove our worth, or he will report us to Malik's father back home. Then we will be sent back in disgrace."

Parvez thought it did not matter about the phones the man knew nothing of them, so it was an easy story to tell. It made him look weak, hopefully saving his life. Who would kill a weak fool?

Brody listened with interest. So he knew where the phones came from now, he just didn't know what was going to happen. He also knew that the Palestinian Liberation Army and his new friend Abdi were working together in some kind of joint operation. The question was, would this be enough information to get someone higher in the food chain willing to listen and take action? He seriously doubted it. His years of collecting intel around the world meant he knew what was expected. This was flimsy at best, but he had to try.

Parvez apparently did not know any-more about the plan. Brody asked him about his team. There were six of them with the leader being Malik. Apart from that, they had trained in the deserts in urban warfare, weapons, and general insurgent strategy skills: bomb-making, taking hostages and the like.

Parvez was the usual follower in these types of things. His brother had introduced him to Malik about a year ago. Malik had convinced him to join and go to the desert. He did not really know why he was there, he just had brothers in arms, and a reason to get up in the morning. Now he found himself terrified, with no control over his own destiny.

Brody reached around Parvez's throat with his forearm. Before the young soldier could make a sound, the oxygen to his brain was cut off and he lay unconscious. Brody needed twenty minutes to make his escape. The body was limp in his arms, the boy's pulse was still beating softly, he was fit! Parvez would wake up in about half an hour with a splitting headache and a lot of shame. Then he would hopefully go back to his bed and try his best to forget all about his trip to the latrine.

Brody crept back to the gate and climbed silently over. He collected his gear in the crevice of the channel and swam back out through the reef and into the inky ocean once again. He surfaced on the ocean side of the dhow. Hassan and Gumbao were waiting in the darkness for him.

Once he was on board, *Shukran* headed directly out to sea to get some distance from the beach, then back towards the entrance to Mtwappa Creek. As it was a moonless night, they had to rely on Gumbao up on the bow and the instruments to successfully enter the narrow channel. When they crossed the reef line into the calm waters of the creek, the crew finally relaxed. Another mission accomplished without problems. The dhow idled along the creek in the dark. Brody was deep in thought. This was bigger than a few thugs, it was international, and from the intel, well organized.

The dhow hove to at the jetty and docked at 03:00. Brody was way too full of adrenaline to sleep. He was always so pumped up at the end of a mission. With nothing else on offer, he headed over to the Full Moon Bar to see if a drink could be found. Barry was just telling the staff to close up for the night. There had been a small birthday party. A few of the last remaining guests were still drinking whiskey at a table, fighting off the end of the party as hard as they could.

Barry waved Brody over and they sat down to a drink. The night was hot and humid. The air seemed charged like a thunderstorm was brewing. But it was probably the excess energy running through his body as it slowly reset itself to normality. A couple of beers would help the process.

The Special Boat Operator side of his mind was ticking like a clock, analyzing everything that had been seen and heard during the incursion into enemy territory: the thoughts, the assumptions, discarding the unrealistic and cementing the real facts into his brain. The brutal truth was that no one around here would take him seriously. These people had some clout in the neighborhood. If he started shouting. They would just have him disappeared and that would be the end of it.

He thought back to his days in the Special Boat Service. His sergeant on the last mission into Somalia had been a good friend, they had worked together for over ten years. Brody remembered it like it was yesterday. Dave was a solid guy, he had left the service not long after Brody. But he had stayed in the UK and gotten married to a young girl from the south of England. Brody had spoken to him a couple of times on the phone after he had left, Dave had asked for advice on what to do, but Brody had been pretty useless on the matter as he hardly knew what to do himself. Dave had wandered around from job to job for a while, then ended up, as so many ex-soldiers do, in a private security company. Last Brody had heard from Dave, which was about nine months ago, he was headed off back to the sandpit to do some private close security work. Dave had explained that his wife was not happy about it as she married him because he had left the Navy, but they had a kid coming and sitting at home did not pay the bills, so he was back at it. If he was back from the middle east then he might have some contacts. All of this was spinning around in his brain, being sorted into useful and no useful tactical information.

Brody enjoyed a couple of beers and went back to *Shukran* for a short sleep. Before dawn, he had to be up again. Hopefully, in the cold light of the early morning, he could come up with a realistic plan of action. The situation was getting way too serious.

Chapter Seven

Abdi walked from the early morning prayer. It was 04:00, the prayer was always short at this time. The calling was for the truly devoted, those few who would get up early every day to greet Allah.

His small troop of six soldiers from Palestine were dutifully falling in behind him. They had not proven to be such a sound investment. Abdi had spent a lot of time with Malik's father in Palestine working through the details of their plan. Malik was not his father. He was a pale reflection of him, but Abdi had to make the best of the situation.

The day before, when Bashir had made the telephone call, Abdi could not believe these stupid children could have made such a mistake. As punishment for this serious crime, he had stopped the meeting with Muna, his lifelong friend from Old Town Mombasa, who was the mastermind behind the attack. The telephones could so easily give the game away. All it took was one mistake, and all would be lost. After calming down a little and drinking some tea, he had walked with Malik out into the garden and had him explain his shameful episode in Malindi.

Now, thankfully, all was back on track. During prayer, Abdi had been carefully watching the group of so-called soldiers. The one named

Parvez looked pale and sick, as if he had not slept. Abdi decided that from now on the team would work out in the compound to keep their minds off the mission.

He only needed them for a little while longer, then they would all end up in paradise as the clerics told them. Meeting Allah in the Garden of Eden and receiving seventy-two virgins each. Such crap! Abdi had been a realist for most of his life. Getting the Christians out, and the Jews as well if he could, this was his only goal. But going to Heaven with virgins, that was just twaddle to get stupid youngsters to pick up a gun or wrap explosives around their waists. Well, better some useless Palestinians than his African boys and girls.

The plan was straightforward and direct. He had spent months developing the idea with Muna, now they were on the brink of success. The stupid boys with the telephone had caused a problem. Then when he had sent some of his men to get the phone and the culprit back, they had been beaten. It sounded very much like the guy that Barry had brought. But why would he be in some whore bar, selling alcohol? Barry never went to those places.

The second phone was still an issue, but Malik had sworn to him that there was no way of linking it to them. It just spoke of bomb-making and explosions nothing to do with a time or a place. Was

Malik lying? He had kept the story about the phones a secret so why not this?

Abdi was also feeling bad he had sold the weapons to this Brody guy. He wished now he had not. His own greed and vanity had made him show the guns and then sell some worthless pieces to this mzungu for way over the market price. Abdi admonished himself. This was not the way of a good Muslim, he must pray harder and think faster. They were not long away from seeing their plan come to fruition. Then they would disappear into the night and turn up somewhere else, the six boys would be martyrs' to the Muslim faith, and all would be balanced again.

Brody woke at first light. He was up and running along the sand, pushing himself, as usual, trying to get that little bit more from his body. Always push. You never know what your body is capable of if you do not keep on moving the boundaries. Every day he would find a new obstacle: the soft punishing sand or jumping across the tangled mangrove roots, even running through the shallow water. He remembered his basic training when the staff sergeant's job was to break the raw recruits down to nothing, then build them up to more than they were before. The tough old sergeant major had crushed them with grueling marches, runs, and punishments for not shining their boots or not standing straight enough for him. He had shouted in Brody's face, "DO, DON'T THINK! JUST

DO!" That was the mantra of the Marines. Everyone, without exception, must follow orders never think, just do. When he was told to march, he marched. If he was told to run then run. The recruits would be puking their guts up by the side of the road in the pouring rain, with 50lb packs on their backs after running ten long miles. The Staff Sargent would come and shout, "Brody, I never told you to stop! Run! Do not think! Run! Run!"

Brody smiled to himself. That had been a long time ago. Now he beat himself with the same mantra. He powered the last two miles back to *Shukran*, then swam out to the yacht and back, ready for his second coffee of the morning.

Later, standing on the bow of the beautiful wooden dhow, Brody was holding the new telephone up as high as he could, twisting this way and that.

Hassan came up behind him. "Eh. Bwana, what you doing?"

Brody looked at him with a scowl, "Jambo, Hassan. I am trying to get this bloody phone to work. It gets a signal, then when I ring it drops off straight away."

"You ringing that Kikuyu girl?" He said with a sly grin.

Brody replied, with a smile, "No, I want to call the U.K. To talk to a friend of mine."

Hassan looked at him, "You're joking with me. Do you know where you are in this world?"

Brody stopped, "What do you mean? A bloody telephone is a telephone. It calls people, that's its job right?"

Hassan laughed. "Boss, this is Kenya. Not your place. Our government is strict, they won't just allow any Tom, Dick, or Harry to call their friend in another country. You must be mad."

Brody said, "What?"

Hassan looked at Brody as if he was a young kid, "Our government has strict rules. We have only seen your dollars on the street for a few years. It was illegal to carry foreign currency only a while back. Every call you make outside of the country must be logged at a G.P.O. You will need your passport and a good reason." He laughed at the stupid Muzungu.

Brody asked, "So what do I do, smart ass?"

Hassan continued in his kindergarten teacher voice, "You go to the General Post Office, the GPO, then you ask for the Telephone Section. You find them and ask to book a call. Then you fill in the forms, hand over your passport, and wait, and wait. The officials will call you when a slot has been allocated."

Brody looked at him, "What the hell. This place is mad sometimes."

He could see why Mwangi felt he could make a killing on selling mobile phones if the government loosened the laws a little!

It was not far to the GPO and it was still early. The sun was out, but not punishing them yet. The dry, dusty coral track led past houses and streets in a long, winding path until it met the main road. He wandered up to the main drag. It was still the same as usual: the road was as busy as ever, container lorries heading north and south or just pulled into makeshift laybys, the drivers getting breakfast and whatever else they wanted or needed before their long journey ahead.

Small cafes lined the side of the road, four poles hammered into the ground with corrugated sheets above to keep the rain off and offer some shade. Ladies with babies on their backs squatted in the dry dirt with open charcoal fires making hot sweet tea and Mahamry, a deep-fried pastry. After placing his order and taking a seat on a low trestle bench, he sat with his tea and cake, watching the world go by, deep in thought, considering options. From the corner of his eye, he spotted a long pair of gorgeous legs heading his way. They were naked to the thigh, then scantily covered with a thin white skirt. They were followed by a strong, muscular torso, a smile that you could lose yourself in, and dark brown, liquid eyes he knew people would fight wars over.

Wanjiku had found him. She was like a secret agent. He would be somewhere, and suddenly she would be there too.

He smiled, "Hi, how are you today?"

She grinned back, "I'm good, Mr Brody. What you up to? You should not eat here, they never change the oil in the pan," Wanjiku said with a pretty, turned-up nose.

Brody finished his cake and tea, "I'm making a call to a friend in the U.K. Can you show me the General Post Office?"

Wanjiku agreed, "Come with me. I know a girl there, she can help us. But don't you get any ideas, she is beautiful but not as smart as me."

Brody promised he would keep his eyes off the new girl as they headed off into the town.

Wanjiku led Brody through the twisting streets and markets full of jostling people for about twenty minutes. It was only 10:00, but starting to get hot. His head was burning even through his thick mop of dark hair.

They arrived at a slightly run-down building proudly proclaiming itself with a brightly painted blue and red sign saying 'Posta.' This was the center of Mtwappa, the Post Office and Trading Center. When Mtwappa had been a small village on the outskirts of Mombasa, the building had been its business and cultural center. Now Mtwappa was a large, sprawling metropolis, pushing out from the road in all directions, growing every day, hungry for the needs of the whites and the truckers alike.

Wanjiku said, "Wait here while I find my friend. She is called Emaculata like from the Bible, but she is no Christian." She laughed at her own joke!

Wanjiku disappeared inside for ten minutes, then came out with a young woman. Brody was taken aback. This girl was a good six feet tall, probably more. She was thin and shapely with flawless skin that was so black it was almost purple. Emaculata had long, muscular arms, an elegant neck, which led to a strong chin, high, sharp cheekbones, and huge, golden-brown eyes. Her smile, like Wanjiku's, was extreme, he just could not help smiling back. Brody was speechless. Two beautiful girls were stood talking to him. He could hardly believe his luck!

Wanjiku punched him in the ribs, "I told you, keep your eyes on me. Emaculata is my friend, she has no business with you."

Emaculata laughed, "Hey, Mr Brody, pleased to meet you." She held out her long, slim hand to shake his.

Then said, "So, Mr Brody, you want to make an international call." Brody nodded, he was still having problems getting words out.

Wanjiku took over, "Yes, he needs to contact the U.K. How long will it take to get the call?"

Emaculata replied, "He can come with me and wait. Our offices are at the back. He can sit while I talk to the International Operator in Nairobi."

Wanjiku sneered, "You think I am a dumb ass. I will be there too, I'm not leaving this 'Muzungu' in your hands for a minute!"

Emaculata laughed again like she seemed to do it a lot, "OK girl, just come, no problem."

Brody followed two sexy wiggling backsides into the labyrinth of run-down offices. There were piles of folders and files all over the floor. A lazy fan circled overhead for no apparent reason. The battered and scarred desks looked colonial they were so old. Telephone wires were hanging from the ceiling all around the rooms they walked through. Emaculata led them to the back of the building. She sat in an office with four other people: two older ladies and two fat men. These were the controllers of the international telephone lines out of Mtwappa. Brody would have had to pay dearly to get to them, let alone make a call. He suddenly realized this was like a cartel. If you had a position or status, you used it for all it was worth.

Emaculata went to one of the older ladies. She spoke in Swahili for a while, then another language Brody did not understand. Wanjiku whispered in his ear. "That's Jalou from the lake. Her tribe is Luo, that's why she is so tall. They are fisherman and walkers. The Lou walked all the way from the Sudan until they found the lake, then stayed there. We are better. We are farmers and business people. The Kikuyu are workers, the Lou's are tall and arrogant."

Emaculata came back, saying, "Sit, my sister over there will help us. She says ten dollars to make the call, then you have ten minutes at a dollar a minute." Brody paid in advance, then handed over the number to Emaculata and waited.

The phone was ringing. Brody actually felt nervous. When the other end picked, it was a female voice, Brody asked, "Hi, this is William Brody. Can I speak to Dave please?"

The person on the other end said, "Major Brody. We have not heard from you in ages. Must be over a year, Dave is at work, I can give him your number." It was Dave's wife Pauline, Brody guessed.

Brody said, "Thanks, Pauline, much appreciated. I have a pen."

Pauline read the number out, then asked after his health, before they hung up.

Brody looked back to Emaculata, "I need to call this number now." Emaculata went through the same routine, another ten dollars changed hands, and another call was made.

The call was ringing, and Brody was waiting. On the third ring, it picked up. Brody asked for Dave, he was told to hold on. He sat and listened to Beethoven as his one dollar disappeared, then another dollar, and another. Finally, he heard a familiar voice on the other end, "Hi, this is Dave Jones, who am I speaking to?"

Brody smiled, "Hi, Dave, it's Brody. How are you?"

Dave was shocked, "Bloody hell, mate, where did you wash up?"

Brody said, "I am in Kenya, living the dream!"

Dave laughed, "You always said that's what you would do. Fair play. What can I do for you? It's been ages, must be a year or so."

Brody quickly answered the questions and got over the niceties of old Navy buddies meeting up so he could move onto the real reason for his call.

"So, mate, what can I do for you today?" Dave said.

"I have a problem here. I've come across some trouble, and it is more than I can deal with. I'm in a place called Mtwappa near Mombasa. I think there is some sort of terrorist plot and it is too big for me. There're Palestinians involved as well as some Muslims here in Kenya. Do you know anyone in Mossad or the Brits who deal with this kind of thing?" Brody broke off.

"Shit, man, trust you to get yourself involved with terrorist's plots. You could find trouble in a bloody monastery. I spent a bit of time in Israel last year. The wife went mad, but the money was good. Give me an hour and call me back, I will have a name for you," Dave said.

Brody thanked him, and they hung up.

Brody waited his hour and called back. Dave had some good news, there was a group of Mossad currently helping the Kenyan Government with the borders. The military advisors were in Mombasa Port working with the Navy. Dave had arranged for Brody to meet the Colonel in charge later in the day at 16:00. Dave explained he had laid on the fact that Brody was a Special Boats Service Major so the Mossad guys would take them both seriously. The meeting was arranged that afternoon at the Castle Hotel on Moi Avenue in Mombasa.

Brody arrived early at the Castle Hotel. Out of habit, he cased the place first, choosing a seat in back where there were shadows, making sure he could watch both exits simultaneously.

The place was once a colonial hotel: high ceilings with white fans spinning, an open terrace with tables one side of the central aisle and comfortable chairs on the other. Lots of old men sat around chatting and drinking tea or if they were on the easy chairs, smoking and drinking whiskey.

He was sat outside the bar in the corner away from the noise, but able to listen and see what was going on. Brody decided to order a Tusker to blend in, making sure that the barman knew it had to be a cold one. The barman bustled off to the old, highly-polished, wooden bar covered in brass fittings set next to him. Brody could imagine the captains and railway engineers using the bar in the long-gone halcyon days of the British Empire. He sat and watched and waited, slowly sipping his ice-cold lager. At 16:04, Brody saw two obviously military men walk into the hotel lobby from the street. They were solidly built guys, who did not enjoy wearing civilian clothes but had tried their best. It was just another uniform, to be worn in a regulation way. The agents were both dressed exactly the same: blue jeans, a light blue, button-down shirt, and soft-soled leather shoes. With wraparound sunglasses for effect. If they had put a sign up or arrived in a tank, it would not have made much difference. The area was busy, with the restaurant selling food and the bar doing a roaring trade at 16:00. Brody let them wander around for a couple of minutes, then stood up and caught the eye of one of the men. The two agents walked calmly over and sat at the table.

Brody introduced himself, purposefully leaving his army rank out. The first man, and apparently the boss, said his name was Colonel Rabi, and his colleague was a case officer named Madani once this was over, and tea had been brought, they continued.

Colonel Rabi said, "So, Major Brody, our friends in the U.K. say you have some valuable intel for us."

Brody felt and could see from Rabi's body language that he was not taking this very seriously.

But he started anyway, "I have been here for several weeks and have found out something I believe is interesting, and you guys should be looking into it."

Colonel Rabi said, "We have heard you found a telephone with some messages on it. Can we see it?"

Brody handed the telephone over to the Major who passed it to Madani. He flicked it open and proceeded to switch it on.

"Major Brody, why do you think there is an imminent threat here? I know you were in the SBS and a highly-decorated officer, but times have changed since you were in the field."

Colonel Rabi stopped and looked at Brody. He was sizing him up, seeing if he was dealing with a lunatic dodging shadows in the dark.

Brody started by explaining the compound in Kikambala, but left out Barry and the guns Then went his conversation with Parvez and described his visit to the compound in detail, and finished with the Amir, Bashir part of the story. As he was talking, it was clear that Colonel Rabi was not that interested. This had been a courtesy call just to maintain relationships in the U.K.

When he had finished his report, Madani spoke. "This telephone only has numbers from Palestine and Lebanon. It talks of explosions and guns and training, but nothing about Kenya. This is useful. We'll follow up the numbers. Mossad might be able to get some arrests from this."

Colonel Rabi continued, "This is fascinating, Major Brody, thanks. We'll follow up on the numbers. But as you can see there is nothing about Kenya. The Palestinians have very little to do with East Africa. There are a few hotels on the coast but, nothing big. Right now we are just about to start celebrating Hanukkah, so all Jews will be with their families. It's only us working abroad that will not be at home. We will have to find some local place where Jews congregate, which will be difficult!"

Brody said, "Look, this is serious. Why would they secretly bring a group from Palestine into Kenya? There must be something to it."

Colonel Rabi said, "There could be a hundred reasons for that. Drugs, guns, a big deal that they do not want anyone to hear about, many things happen. That alone is an offense, but not a terrorist crime and certainly not under our jurisdiction."

Brody knew they were brushing him off. He was a washed-up old soldier that was now a beach bum. He even looked like one, with his long hair, blue jeans, open shoes, and T-Shirt. About as far away from an S.B.S major as you could get. These guys thought he was a lunatic looking for attention.

Colonel Rabi finished the conversation with, "Here is my card. This is my Kenyan number, call me if you find out anything substantial. Thank you for the phone, it will be useful in our investigations. We'll contact you if anything about Kenya turns up. Happy Hanukkah, Major Brody."

With that, they got up and left. Brody was pissed. He had not learned anything and been treated like a fool. There was definitely something going on. It would happen soon. Just where and when were the questions. The waiter came around and asked if there was anything else. He ordered another beer and watched the crowd grow thicker as the evening wore on. As the beers flowed, his mind kept wandering back to the facts at hand. The S.B.S.

were not investigators. His team had been called in when the higher-ups knew who the bad guys were. The missions were simple: go in and either catch or dispatch the enemy. But when he had attained the rank of major there had been many briefings, lots of intel to sift through. During this time, Brody had picked up some skills and learned that his gut was a good indicator of trouble. And now it was screaming. After an hour, he caught a Matatu back to Mtwappa and headed for the Full Moon Bar.

Abdi was sat in the wide-open living room of his house in Kikambala. On his right sat Muna, his best friend and ally. The six Palestinians sat on his left in a semi-circle with Malik at the front. Further to his right were four Al-Shabab soldiers, who had arrived from the Somalian border earlier in the day.

Their plan was coming together; it had taken a long time. Almost four years had gone by since Muna had approached him with the cunning idea. Together, Muna and Abdi had convinced the Palestinian Liberation Army that a blow to the Jews was important. He wanted them out of East Africa, back in their godforsaken country where they could rot.

The two Freedom Fighters, as they liked to be known, had worked together for many years. Muna was a radical cleric in town who wanted the Kenyan Government to stand up and respect the Sharia law as it should. Their ingenious plan was simple, the

Al-Shabab wanted to stop the tourists coming. This was always their first step to taking over a region: strangle it financially. Then use the word of Islam to convince the youth, who had no jobs due to the lack of hotels, that extreme religion was the answer to their problems. It was like taking candy from a baby. Just look at the six Palestinian fools in front of him, kids with a whole life ahead of them, now tricked into carrying bombs and shooting guns at their assumed enemy. These young boys would all die.

The ruthless plan had been devised with a possible silver lining. The Palestinians would attack the hotel from the front, a car suicide bomb with two operatives, the names of the lucky ones would be held until the last minute. The other four would attack after the bomb had gone off, herding the guests to the rear of the hotel. Once they pushed them out to the beach, another force of Al-Shabab would land with boats and take the visitors away as hostages. They would sell the Jews for diamonds. The idea made Abdi happy: he knew how much the Jews loved their stones.

The Palestinians would most likely die in the fighting. If any managed to survive then the beach party were under strict orders to kill them on site. They were to be left behind, on the beach, to carry the blame for the attack.

Abdi and Muna would make a strike for Islam and at the same time make some good money from the ransom payments.

He explained to the group in front of him, "You, Malik, and your team will be in charge of the hotel. This is the most dangerous part of the operation, and must be handled professionally. Your father has sent you to me for this task, you must not fail in your duty."

Two of the loyal soldiers you have brought to us will be blessed with taking the bomb to the enemy. The chosen ones will drive right up to the entrance and as far inside as the vehicle will go. Once there, they will detonate the bomb, wreaking havoc, sacrificing themselves to kill as many infidels as possible, dying for the one true religion. This is an honor to any true Muslim. Allah will be waiting for you in paradise, the virgins ready for your arrival.

The other four soldiers will enter the hotel earlier and hide among the crowds of holidaymakers. We have arranged for your weapons to be smuggled in and hidden. When the bomb goes off, your task will be to shoot the infidels, but not all of them, push the fools to the beach. I will have boats waiting, get as many Jews on the boats as possible, then make your escape with my men.

Malik replied, "*Shukran*, thank you for your blessing. My team will not fail you. We will strike a blow for Islam and stop the Jews from leaving their shitty country. After our victory, they will be too scared to even leave their filthy homes."

Abdi looked at his four Al-Shabab soldiers. These were his men. "You men will go to the chosen location at the end of the creek. This is a dangerous mission. You will shoot the returning airline as it takes off. We have the heat-seeking missiles. You will take the four by four to the end of Mtwappa Creek. The location has been scouted already. When the aircraft is directly overhead. Release the missiles as you have been shown. The Strela Ground to Air are heat-seeking and find the target, tearing the aircraft and the Jews to pieces. Once you have seen the explosion, make good your escape to Somalia. I'm sorry you cannot be on the main assault, but your work is important."

Abdi wanted no harm to come to his soldiers. His Al-Shabab were better than the Palestinian scum. They should die for Allah, his boys would return home as heroes.

Abdi turned to Malik, "You should now pray and prepare yourselves for battle. Your people must be ready to enter Heaven to meet Allah." They all chanted Allah Akbar, Allah Akbar.

The meeting broke up. Only Abdi and Muna knew the exact date, time, and location of the attack. This would be kept a secret until the last minute.

Chapter Eight

Brody arrived at the Full Moon Bar later that evening. After thinking through the events of the afternoon, it was clear Barry had to be brought up to date. The shit was definitely going to hit the fan in the next couple of days. If this whole affair backfired, Abdi would come looking for Barry and revenge. Brody sat at the bar nursing a beer, considering his options.

The restaurant was full, the locals and tourists coming out for a fish meal under the moonlight, the creek lazily passing by, on its way to pour out into the Indian Ocean. There were occasional calls from the night birds, and cicadas screeching in the bush around the bar, a wonderful way to spend a tropical evening. The heat was increasing steadily. It was mid-November, the hot, dusty wind was coming from the north-east, the Kaskazi, right off the Indian Sub-Continent. Humidity reached into the high nineties, especially close to the creek, with temperatures getting to 100 degrees Fahrenheit at times. During the evening, the wind only came in light, refreshing puffs, just enough to appreciate, then it was gone, the heat descending once more like a hot wet blanket covering everything.

Barry wandered over and sat on a barstool, "Hey, mate, what's wrong? You look down in the dumps, not living the dream?"

Brody knew he had to tell Barry straight out or he would never manage, "Barry, I have something to say to you."

"Well go on, mate, spit it out. It can't be all that bad," Barry replied.

Brody explained the events of the last week, everything from the telephones to the bar fight to the mosque to Abdi's compound and even the Mossad agents in town. When he finally finished, Barry said, "Shit, mate, let's get a round in, I think we need it!"

Brody took his cold beer gratefully and waited. Barry said, "Mate, do you believe that this is terrorism. I know you were in the navy and stuff so I would trust you. You Poms always have an ear for that kinda stuff, what with the IRA and all."

Brody said, "This is trouble. I can sense it. My gut is telling me some serious shit is going to hit the fan, and soon. I just don't know when or where."

Barry answered, "Mate, that Abdi guy is bad news. I dealt with him for my own protection. There's no love lost between us. If he is some Al-Shabab then I'm against him. I've lived here for ages now and don't want my life messed up by some crappy rag head on a mission."

Brody laughed, "Not technically a rag head, but close enough."

Barry said, "Well, you know what I mean, don't you, buggers messing up everything? This place is hard enough without bloody bombs going off left right and center. So, mate, what's the plan?"

Brody knew Barry was in. He was a sailor, not a soldier, but he was at least on their side, for moral support, if nothing else.

Brody explained, "Tomorrow night I am going back into meet my friend Parvez, he is a weak link. If I can get him alone, and make some sort of deal, then maybe I can get more information."

Barry said, "Good on you mate, let me know if I can help. Don't worry about Abdi and my gun supplies that's easy, I can always find another there are hundreds of them in Mtwappa."

The following morning, after Brody's run and a very early breakfast, *Shukran* was fired up and headed out to sea. He wanted to do an offshore reccee. They left the entrance to Mtwappa Creek behind them and entered the long slow swells of the Indian Ocean. Once clear of the final reef outcrops, Brody and Gumbao hauled the boom to the top of the mast, pulled the sail, attached it to the stern gunwale, and sat back to enjoy the slow, peaceful march into the ocean. The sea was calm, blue, and looked like it went on forever. They sailed on, enjoying the wind in the sails and the slow rising and falling that is sailing, on and on, never-ending. *Shukran* was a good sailing craft holding the wind well, she was a fat-bellied dhow, so did not list overly as the sail pulled them through the water. The day was beautiful, they sailed on until the boiling hot sun was overhead. The sky was cobalt blue and clear not a cloud in sight, a perfect day. The deck became so hot only Gumbao could walk on it. His feet probably had no feeling left. He didn't seem to notice as he wandered around tightening lines and checking the rudder, always on the lookout for Mother Nature to throw a spanner in the works.

Shukran had been sailing for several hours, the coast of East Africa slowly disappearing behind them. Finally, at the twelve-mile mark, there was no sign of land. The main shipping routes into Mombasa Port were very close. The crew could see massive ships carrying hundreds of containers stacked four and five deep on their long decks.

Hassan said, "We must steer clear of those ships. It takes them hours and miles to stop or change course. The swell, if we are within a mile or so, can tip *Shukran* over in the water, the crew on the container vessel would never even notice."

Gumbao agreed, "I had a friend off the coast at Tiwi Beach fishing the passage into the harbor, in a skiff. He went out one night, then just disappeared for days. After about a week. He turned up in Lamu. His boat had been overturned and he had sat on top of it for five days eating flying fish!"

They carried on chatting, dozing, and enjoying the day.

At 15:00, Brody was considering heading back. He had thought through his problem, and now had a clear plan. The day in the ocean had cleaned his brain. The clarity had come back. He knew what to do and how to do it. The only problem was the where and the when. As they were coming about, getting ready to head back towards the coastline some fifteen miles away, Brody spotted a small fishing boat on the horizon. It caught his eye, as it was towing four smaller boats behind.

After checking it out with the binoculars, he could see no fishing nets in the water, and the four boats just sat behind the main craft. The fishing vessel was about eighty feet long, with a high rear cabin. The three boats being towed looked like fiberglass inshore speed boats, with large outboards on the back, something like 150HP, but it was hard to make out at this distance. During Brody's training, he had seen setups like this. The pirates used them. The fishing boat was the mother ship, and the fast speed boats did the dirty work, chasing the tankers, trying to board them and take over the crew. Once boarded, the ships would be sailed to a nearby port and ransomed back to their owners.

Hassan had noticed, "Boss, this is not a good place to be, we should get out of here, you are a 'Muzungu.' That means ransom to those guys."

Gumbao said, "Shall I get the guns from below?"

Brody thought for a second, "No. Let's just make a run for it and get out of here as fast as we can."

Shukran was tacked and headed back the way she had come, sailing towards the coast. Brody spent the time preparing for the night dive back to Abdi's compound. He was sure by now most of the plan would have been revealed to the group. The idea was to sneak in, grab Parvez again, then get enough information out of the scared kid to stop this nightmare from going ahead. He was sure the plot was imminent. The Palestinians had not been brought here to wait around. The operation would probably go ahead in less than ten days after their arrival.

Brody had filled his tank back up to 3000psi and checked his equipment thoroughly the day before. He had then cleaned the Glock, making sure the magazine was full.

Now all there was to do was wait. They wanted to get near to Abdi's compound around 22:00. As they approached in the same way as before, Brody got ready for his second-night dive. The moon was only a sliver in the night sky, hardly any light at all. The stars were full. Without the moon's glow on its surface, the sea was pitch black, almost sinister, daring him to enter. The instruments glowed faintly red from the stern cabin but were almost invisible. All other lights were extinguished. The large dhow sat in the water motionless. She was invisible unless you knew where to look, only then could you see the vague outline, like a ghost ship.

Brody took a giant stride off the ocean side of *Shukran*, then slowly sank towards the bottom. The water was dark and enveloping, the stars disappeared as he descended into the depths, the dive gauges on his arm glowing a pale alien green. At thirty-feet, the alarm beeped. This was the signal to blow some air into his buoyancy jacket, arresting the descent. Everything was all right so far. He switched on the small torch to look around. It was eerie in the underwater silence. All he could hear was his own deep, slow breaths, the bubbles like silver mushrooms gliding to the surface. With no time to lose, he switched the dive computer to compass mode. The glowing points appeared with the small rectangular box in the bottom of the screen set to the same bearing as before. Once again, he set off into the darkness, counting his fin strokes. He knew it had been eighty-four last time. He moved through the water as quickly as possible, heading for the reef. Brody could not see the bottom but used the depth gauge to maintain thirty feet. Using long easy strokes, he was eating up the distance, then suddenly an ice-cold chill ran down his spine. Something else was in the water nearby.

He knew there were fish around him, but this was different. Something bigger. It passed again, gliding through the water in silence. Feeling his stomach lurch, he swam deeper to forty feet, but it followed, getting closer with every pass. The wash from the flick of a tail somewhere off in the dark pushed him through the water. Then his tank was hit, something knocked it and disappeared into the void. Brody knew the only thing to do was head for the bottom. Going to the surface made him a sitting duck. The ocean was full of predators much higher than him on the food chain.

He sensed the next attack before it hit. His tank was grabbed by massive jaws and dragged for a second then let go. As the air cylinder was spat, out a soulless black eye passed him. Brody went straight for the bottom, dumping the air from the jacket and landing on the sand with a thump. Looking around, he was on the rocky sand about fifty feet underwater with nowhere to go. His torch only penetrating about ten feet, at times like this his brain just switched to a machine: no panic, no fear, just animal instincts. The survival of the fittest. He kept a lookout all around and started finning across the broken bottom towards the reef and the rocks, looking for some cover. His lungs were heaving now, swallowing and gulping down the air. The next attack came from above. It was hard and fast, hitting the tank slamming, him into the sand and rocks on the bottom, then grinding him through the debris for some twenty feet, knocking the wind out of his lungs. Then it was gone silence as quickly as it had arrived. The bull shark swam off into the night. It either thought he was another predator entering his patch or dinner!

After getting his breath back, he continued along as fast as he could. The huge predator swam at him again, this time from the other side. Brody rolled as the shark came in. He took the regulator out of his mouth and sent a blast of air into the shark's snout, sending it reeling away, confused for a second.

The thing was not done. It swam off into the darkness to recover. Brody was almost at the reef. He could see the entrance and the loose boulders from the dynamite. He raced towards the largest one. The shark came back into the torch beam, and headed straight for Brody. He ducked under a rough coral block as the shark hit the other side, rolling it across the sea bottom. Brody was fighting for his life. This predator had the edge here and would wear Brody out very quickly.

The giant fish swam back off into the night. Brody sat panting on the seafloor, trying to get his breath under control. The water was much shallower in the entrance to the passageway, only twenty feet, his air should last ages at this depth. However, conservation was always a priority. If he did not get to the surface quickly, the return trip would be precarious.

The shark came again, fast and strong, it grabbed Brody's tank in its jaws and started swimming across the bottom. Brody twisted, he could only do one thing. As the shark continued swimming, thrashing its prey against the rocks, trying to kill it, Brody struggled but could not break free from the vice-like grip. He twisted in his jacket, reaching inside and trying to unzip the pocket. His fingers got torn away, again and again. His mask twisted and filled with water. Finally, the zip moved, sliding open. His fingers felt inside for the plastic bag. Pulling it out, the smooth material slipped from his fingers as the shark threw him in the water then smashed him to the bottom. His eyes glazed as he was pushed again, sliding along, he grabbed the plastic bag as it slid underneath him. Pointing the bag at the shark's head, he pulled the trigger. He was at almost point-blank range, but the bullet from his Glock had to travel through water, not air, which is much denser. The bullet left the barrel inside the bag at the standard velocity, but as soon as it hit the water it started to slow down. He could almost see it in the torchlight.

The round went straight into the shark's mouth, the weakest part of this massive animal. It must have penetrated something as it threw Brody away as if a bee had stung it. It twisted in the water. As it did, Brody could see a small hole in its upper jaw with ragged skin hanging from it. The shark turned towards the ocean and was gone. Brody stopped, then raced to the channel and swam as quickly along it as he could. Once he found his crevice, he sat on the bottom in twelve feet of pitch-black water with his torch off and breathed. He sat in the same position, until his heart stopped trying to break through his chest. Continuously keeping an eye out for the shark down the channel. The enormous predator did not like creatures that fought back. It was a fast, emotionless killer that did not want to fight. Brody had put up too much of a battle.

When his breathing had returned to normal, and the dive equipment was safely stored, he moved to the surface. All was silent as before. He left the ocean quickly, then climbed the gate into the compound and dodged through the shadows moving with purpose. It was much easier this time, he knew where to go. In a few moments, he had reached the small windows for the accommodation block. The first three were occupied, there were two more left to try to get hold of Parvez. Brody peered into the last window. The room was in darkness, but there were soft sounds of a person deep in sleep. A body was lying on a bed on the far wall. Brody carefully climbed in through the window. The room was hot, the air was wet with moisture. Silently crossing the small space, he moved over to the sleeping figure, then purposefully clamped the mouth and nose, holding Parvez down with his body weight.

Parvez's eyes opened in panic, he could not breathe. He saw Brody above him. The memories of a few nights ago raced through his brain. Had this guy come back to kill him after all? Parvez did not struggle. He knew he was done for. He deserved this fate, Allah was annoyed with him.

Brody motioned for him to be silent. Parvez nodded his agreement, happy to have a few more seconds of life using sign language, Brody instructed him to get up and head back to the latrine. He was taking a risk letting him walk down the corridor and out to the toilet on his own. But he figured the guy was scared. And if he raised the alarm now it would look very bad. It was worth it to find out the information, time was not standing still.

Brody went out of the window and waited beside the wall. The door creaked open after a few moments and Parvez walked out, heading for the small stone building away from the house. Brody followed him in the shadows wondering if he had been betrayed or not. Parvez went behind the small block building. Brody appeared out of the darkness. Parvez's face was glistening with sweat. He was visibly shaking in front of Brody.

Parvez said, "Sir, I have been thinking so much. I do not want to be here. I was misled. I am scared. You have to help me, I cannot stay."

It all came out in a long stream of whispers Parvez was terrified of what he had gotten himself into. It had all dawned on him during the afternoon meeting. Listening to Abdi, he realized the reality of the situation. His bowels had turned to water, he was so scared he was virtually paralyzed.

Brody said, "If you help me, I will help you. But I need to know all the information you have. If it's good, I will do all that I can to make sure you don't die."

Parvez smiled, "Sir. I will explain all I know. We had a meeting today with Mr Abdi and a Mr Muna. They explained everything to us. All we do not know is the time and the place, but it is very soon."

Brody listened to Parvez as he explained everything to him. Parvez went into every detail he could remember, desperately trying to save his own skin. Brody watched him for lies, but from his body language, he was telling the truth.

It brought back memories of fighting the rebels in Somalia. There had been so many children holding guns that had no idea why they were there or who they were fighting. These kids got dragged in for a bowl of food, then were brainwashed, as there was no other information. After a very short training period, the new soldiers of the revolution found themselves with a machine gun in their hand and an enemy running towards them shooting. The radical clerics had all disappeared, it was just the bullets flying and the bombs exploding. Nowhere to run, so they died in the dust wasted, lost lives.

Brody explained, "Listen, you will have to go back, but I will find you. I will do my best to give you a chance to escape before you have to go into battle."

Parvez was crying now sobbing about his mother and his father, how he would never see them again.

Brody said, "Listen, go back to your room. I will try to find out where and when this will go down. If you run now they will go after your family. We need to finish this properly."

He slipped across the garden and over the gate, Found his equipment and slowly and very cautiously headed out of the channel into the ocean. He swam along the bottom with his nose in the sand, until he was sure he was near *Shukran*, then circling continuously, he slowly surfaced. He was certain the huge shark was approaching so many times. When he finally, safely surfaced, he was totally disorientated and exhausted.

Shukran was about fifty feet further offshore. Brody ducked down and, very slowly so as not to attract attention, swam over to the boat. Once onboard, they set off for Mtwappa. His dive tank was peppered with deep indentations, a reminder of his near miss with the bull shark.

Chapter Nine

Brody woke way before dawn as usual. The weather at this time of year was constant it kept coming wave after wave there was no escape, with the humidity levels never falling below 80%. Down near the water, he was sure it was worse, more like a constant 95%.

Hassan had been up for a while. He was setting out for the first prayer of the day, putting his prayer mat down near the bow of the dhow, facing it carefully towards Mecca, then commencing his morning ritual.

Brody had his morning ritual too. He got dressed and headed out on his run, pushing it as usual to the old tree that marked his two and a half miles. He slogged back through the sand. The burn always felt good. His thighs and calves were on fire as he made the last turn and headed for *Shukran*. Getting back, he immediately stripped off, then dived over the side. The water sent a shiver through his body, although it was around 75 degrees at this time of year. He swam with long, smooth, freestyle strokes out to Barry's yacht, then taking a deep breath and powering twenty feet underwater, finally coming up with a blast to *Shukran*, ready for the new day.

As Brody was eating his Mahamry and drinking coffee, Barry appeared, wearing last night's shirt, crumpled trousers, and with a day's growth on his chin. This was early for him, which was concerning. he typically surfaced around 11:00. Barry came on board and accepted a small cup of strong, sweet, Arabic coffee. They sat for a moment enjoying the brew and the view across the creek. It was so quiet and peaceful. There were a few herons on the opposite side, stalking through the water, looking for small fry. A pied kingfisher was hovering over the middle of the creek, waiting for a fish to stay still long enough to be caught. High in the sky, a black and white fish eagle was flying in long, lazy circles, keeping an eye for any prey that was careless enough to wander into its view.

Barry had a furrowed brow, it was easy to see he had been thinking all night. "Mate. I'm in. When this thing goes down, you have to come find me. We'll deal with it together."

Brody was taken aback. He knew his new friend Barry was a good guy, but this was pushing it. He said. "Thanks. I appreciate that. If there is anything you can help me with, I'll be sure to ask."

Barry just nodded, "Guns, mate, I've guns, what do we need? I've collected several good specimens over the years they're all cleaned and ready for action."

Brody replied, "Brilliant, if we need any I'll let you know, but so far it's the Loner if this all goes down. I can't see how *Shukran* will be of much use."

"She's in, mate, at your disposal. A moment's notice and a push and we'll catch the bastards!"

With that off his chest, Barry got up, slapped Brody on the back, moved his portly body along the gangplank with surprising agility, and was gone.

Abdi was at the compound. There was a mere twenty-four hours before the plan was to be set in motion. Muna had come back from town earlier with the car, a stolen Pajero four-wheel drive. They had taken it from a Muzungu in the South Coast. His house was unoccupied. It probably would not be missed until someone spotted it on T.V.

Abdi asked, "How is the vehicle going?"

Muna said, "My friend. This will be a sight to behold. We have filled the car with Semtex Explosives, stolen from the Army when they were in Somalia teaching us a lesson. Then we have been slowly buying boxes of wood nails, six inches, and four inches. My driver, you know him, Adib, he was a builder of sorts for many years. He suggested we buy masonry nails. These nails are much harder they will fly through the air like a million arrows."

Abdi replied, "Now what do you plan to do with all of this destruction?"

Muna carried on happily, he loved to build bombs, "When the car is in position, the driver will press the detonator. This will explode the fuel tanks and the bomb, we have two extra tanks in the back seat and one in the boot. The car will become an inferno, killing many around it and the roof of the building will catch fire, we hope other areas too. The wind of fire will incinerate anyone nearby. Those Jews will taste Hell a second before they arrive," he finished with a chuckle.

Abdi was keen for the rest of the gruesome story, "Then, my friend?"

"Then, from the fire, a million missiles will come at the speed of light, piercing and penetrating everything in their way, from all directions. It will be like the sun exploding and pouring its wrath onto the unfaithful. No one will survive. If anyone lives through it, they will be burnt and maimed forever."

Abdi sat imagining their plan. The car racing into the foyer of the hotel, smashing the desks and people out of the way, killing the Jews as they stood with their dumb mouths open, staring at death. Then the car stopping, for a moment, silence, everyone thinking they were safe, all of those Jewish idiots, looking at each other, smiling, breathing a deep breath of relief, thinking 'My God, we were lucky!' Abdi could see it clearly in his mind: the happy people rushing forward to find out if they could help. The Jews would find their new happiness short-lived as a massive fireball erupted from the car. It would be like Hell, as it carried thousands of nails shooting through the air like a swarm of locusts blackening the sky. The missiles would impale them, pass through them and kill the person behind them the women and children would all be dead and dying. The place would be engulfed in flames and death, everywhere death. And that would not be the end. His Palestinian Martyrs would rush out and start shooting people, pushing the Jew sheep to the beach, in their panic. Only for more misery to rain down, like their God had turned his back on them.

The second and cleverest part of his plan was the missiles, a pure stroke of genius. The plane would take off from Mombasa Airport, in panic, rushing away from the death and carnage to safety with home in their sights, celebrating their lives, happy they missed the terrible tragedy that befell the new arrivals. Then the plane would reach the end of the runway and take off, lifting its lumbering weight into the sky. His brave soldiers would raise their American weapon of death and simply blow it out of the sky. Hundreds more dead with one shot. They would not know what hit them. The country and city would destroy itself, rioting on the streets, everyone blaming each other. Tourists would not come for years and years.

Then Muna and Abdi would rise as saviors from the ashes, using the ransom money to rebuild the coast. There would be no jobs in the tourist industry. With no wages, the whole region would collapse into a financial meltdown. The central government would cede the coast to the Muslim fathers. With the youth flocking to them, the mosques would be full, finally bringing law and order back to the coast. He would run for president of the new state and win with a landslide victory. All the time using the Jew's money to fund the new State of Islam.

All in all, a perfect plan, and it would start tomorrow. That would be the day of the Holy Holiday, the start of Hanukkah, the Jew's special day when they found some old temple in Jerusalem and called it their own again. On this day, he would kill their faith and chase them back to their stinking country on their knees.

Abdi smiled at his magnificent dream. The path had been laid by Allah for him to follow, he was merely an instrument. His wife had commented as she dressed him the other night, "Abdi, my husband, you look more and more like a president every day, the way you walk and hold yourself a real statesman."

On the morning of 28th November, Brody had enjoyed his run and taken breakfast. He was still worrying about this attack, but all had gone quiet. They could only sit and wait for something, anything to give them a clue. He was considering heading back to the compound that night to see if anything had changed, maybe see if Parvez had any new information he could wring out of him. He had even considered calling the Mossad people, but the Colonel had just blown him off, thinking Brody just saw conspiracy theories, a bored, lost, washed-up marine looking for excitement.

Brody had made sure all the weapons were cleaned and ready, all the magazines were full, the shotgun racked and loaded. Getting more information was imperative now. If this went down and he did not try his best to stop it, he would never forgive himself or the Mossad agents.

Just after 15:00, Brody grabbed a bike and headed for town, going straight to Mwangi's bar. The old man was there, sitting chatting to his old friends. He saw Brody and welcomed him like a long-lost brother. But there was no news, the place was silent. He had asked all his friends and relatives and nothing was going on. Police Corporal Naivasha was sitting with them enjoying a cold beer and some Nyama Choma before heading back out into the heat to annoy the Matatu drivers and get some cash for the evening. It was a kind of tax, he explained to Brody.

"They don't follow the law. But they want to continue driving those heaps of junk. It is my duty as an officer to remove them from the road. But this government does not pay our salaries, so what am I to do? If they ask me to look away, it's only a few shillings, not actually causing any harm."

Finishing his meal of roast meat and beer. He got up without even offering to pay. And left through the kitchen door, then slid his portly belly behind the wheel of his brand-new Toyota Corolla, fresh from Mombasa Port, and drove off.

Wanjiku appeared in the doorway, "Hi," she said. Brody was pleased to see her. She seemed excited about something.

They got a beer and sat at the bar. Wanjiku was dressed perfectly as usual, like she had just left a fashion show. He did not know how she managed to look so good all the time.

Brody asked, "So, what's new?"

Wanjiku replied, "I've a great job tonight. I'm a dancer at a show, they gave me the clothes to wear and everything. I've to stand with the other girls and wiggle my ass, then move around like this." She showed the moves, gyrating her hips around the room.

Brody said, "That's great, you can buy dinner tomorrow then." She laughed and slapped his arm.

"I've to leave in about twenty minutes, or I'll be late, it's out at Kikambala, a hotel there."

Brody went along with the conversation, "What are you dancing for?"

Wanjiku said, "It is more who I am dancing for. There's a group of tourists coming in, they are VIP. The hotel has set up a special welcome, which is me!" She said with a huge smile.

Brody asked, "So what is it then?"

"It's called Hamlick, we're celebrating a Hamlick for the people. That is what the dance is called, the Dance of the Lights."

Brody was not that interested, it did not sound like his kind of thing, and the hotel would not let outsiders in for a special occasion.

They carried on chatting, "I thought you had to leave?"

Wanjiku replied, "I'm waiting for Emaculata, she's meeting me here. Anyway, it's African time, don't worry. You 'Muzungus' always use those watches, we don't need them."

"But the airplane will arrive on time," Brody said.

"Ah, the traffic will sort that problem out. It will be all right. Let's have another beer while we wait for her," she replied.

Brody didn't mind seeing Emaculata's legs again. That would be very enjoyable!

Emaculata finally arrived, looking stunning. She had a white dress on which brought the darkness of her skin out. With her slim but shapely body, Brody had a problem taking his eyes off her. She promptly sat at the bar and ordered a beer. Brody was amazed at how these people did not see or use time as any kind of reference to life.

He said, "Emaculata, how's life? You seem happy today. Are you looking forward to the dancing?"

She smiled. "It's great. My tribe are Nilotic from the lake, so I'm probably related to these guys in some way. We were the ancient pharaoh's children, but we got up and left, walking along the Nile until we got here. Now I am in Mtwappa." She said with a laugh.

Brody caught the historical link and carried it on, "What's the dance you are doing tonight?"

Emaculata replied, "It's the festival of lights, the Jewish ceremony for Hanukkah."

Brody slammed his fist on the table, "Shit! That's it. I know what's going to happen, Shit! Shit! Shit! You cannot go, that's where the bombs are going off! You said there's a plane as well. Parvez said they were going to shoot the plane down too. I saw the ground to air heat-seeking missiles in Abdi's store. Don't go to this thing or you will get blown up. Stay here." With that, he jumped up and ran out of the bar.

Brody ran across the street, jumped on a motorcycle at the taxi stand, and raced off back towards *Shukran* with the angry taxi guy chasing him. He hammered down the dirt tracks, heading for the bar, desperately forming a plan in his head. He skidded to a stop in the car park, dropping the bike on the floor, then racing into the bar and grabbing Barry, "It's on, we got to get the Loner ready. It's in Kikambala at the Peponi Hotel! Take this card, ring the Colonel and tell him to come with all he's got. Tell him their plane heading back is going to be targeted at take-off by a heat-seeking missile based at the end of Mtwappa Creek. Four guys in a four by four!"

Barry leaped up, grabbed the card, and headed for the telephone. Brody ran to *Shukran*.

He was shouting as he ran across the jetty. Hassan and Gumbao came on deck wondering what the problem was. Brody leapt over the gunwale onto the wooden planks of the deck and went straight below, coming up a few seconds later with his seaman's bag. Emptying it onto the bench in the back cabin, he picked up the AK47, passing it to Gumbao, "Do you know how this works?"

Gumbao nodded. Brody gave him the gun, then stood in amazement as Gumbao field stripped the gun in front of him, checked all the moving parts and tested the springs then put it back together again. He tapped the magazine on the deck then slotted it into the gun, like an old pro. Brody was shocked into silence, what the fuck! He made a mental note that one day soon when this was all over, he would sit Gumbao down and find out who the hell this guy was!

He passed out the spare magazines, then collected the Ithaca shotgun and the Glock which were all ready for action. Once the weapons were done with, he explained to Hassan that the boats would probably come into the reef to collect the people off the beach. They should go and try to block their exit. He would come from the beach and try to stop the main attack on the front. Then, if he could, he would attack the Somalis on the beach.

Gumbao listened, and then went to get the boat ready for the sea and battle. Everyone had their jobs to do. Brody untied *Shukran* and set her loose into the creek. With the engines roaring, the dhow headed off as fast as she could into the setting sun.

Brody returned to Barry in the car park. He had managed to get the Loner running and was revving her up. He loaded the pump-action shotgun into the car, then gave Barry the Glock,

"Do you know how to use this?"

Barry replied, "Don't worry mate, I brought me own!" He dragged a massive, polished Ruger Super Redhawk out from beside him. Brody had never seen one before, the weapon had six shots in a revolving chamber. A solid heavy gun that fired either 3" or 2.5" .480 shells. This gun was made to stop things. It was like Dirty Harry's older brother. Brody did not know what to say with his tiny Glock next to this cannon.

He laughed, stuffing the gun in his trousers and said. "Let's Go!"

The Loner raced off down the track. The V8 six-cylinder engine was warmed up, it took off like a bullet from a gun, throwing dust and dirt up as they hammered along the track. There was no slowing for potholes. The old car just rammed through anything that was in the way. Barry had his hand on the horn but it was pretty much drowned out by the noise of the engine. People were diving for cover as the Landrover hared along the twisting road towards Mtwappa, flying out into the traffic of the main road in what seemed like just a few seconds and almost broadsiding a 'Matatu' which blared its horn angrily at them.

Barry kept the old girl under control, turning north and careering off along the road, weaving in and out of the evening traffic as they raced towards Kikambala.

The four-wheel-drive full of Semtex was pulling out through the black gate of the compound. The martyrs were to drive slowly and carefully, not to make any sudden turns or attract any attention what-so-ever, arriving at the hotel after dark. The remaining four Palestinians had been dispatched to the hotel earlier in the day. Abdi's brother, one of the cooks, had helped them get into position away from the foyer, then hidden their weapons close by. Abdi sent his precious Al-Shabab soldiers, armed with the Strela launcher and two missiles, to the exact location at the end of Mtwappa Creek where they would await the airplane. The missiles had cost him dearly, over twenty thousand dollars each, but it was small change in the grand scheme. Now it was in Allah's hands.

He had chosen Parvez and Rafid as the lucky suicide bombers. Parvez was weak and would not shoot the infidels in the hotel, but Rafid was a true believer, keeping Parvez in line, making sure the plan succeeded.

Barry and Brody were hitting over 80 mph in the old 109 V8 Landrover. This was beyond its top speed by almost 20 MPH. These cars were not meant for speed or comfort, it was all about survival with a 109. The leaf springs front and back were not designed to deal with this type of treatment over the rugged, potholed road. The vehicle flew along, bouncing and veering as it landed in one pothole, then was sent careening towards the next. Inside the car was no better. The doors and windows were rattling and shaking off their hinges. The engine was bellowing as Barry fought the beast to keep her on the road, continuously accelerating to pass a slow truck only to have to swerve back into his lane, narrowly avoiding another. The evening was turning into night very quickly. Maybe they would be too late.

The old car was being pushed to its limits, heading the twenty miles north to Peponi Hotel. The sun had set. As always in the tropics, the light was leaving fast, it would be pitch dark in a few minutes. Barry flicked the feeble lights on which just lit the road immediately ahead of them but no more. The squaddies of the British army loved their Landrovers. They always said they were full of character. The wide front wings had been left on purpose by the manufacturers so the soldiers could brew their tea on them. Right now, they could have done with a brand-new Toyota VX eight-cylinder with turbo drive, but the 'Loner' was doing her best, flying blind as a bat, through the night, rattling and shaking as if she was about to disintegrate. When she got past sixty-five miles an hour, the left front wheel got a severe wobble, twisting the steering wheel out of Barry's hands, flinging the car around on the single-lane road. Barry gritted his teeth and pushed the car way past its limits.

Rafid was driving the Pajero at a moderate speed, keeping within the speed limits, not daring to overtake with his precious load. The two suicide bombers had been stuck behind a lorry for most of the way down from the north towards the target. Tonight was his night, time to meet Allah and the virgins. Paradise forever, leaving his earthly body behind. Praying five times a day since his sixth birthday had paid off. The family could not afford food or school, but they prayed every single day without fail. The clerics had spoken to his father and then taken him, saying his son had a special mission for Allah. Rafid smiled. This was it, the special purpose. The clerics had been right, a blow against Jews and Christians.

The clerics had told his father he was a chosen one. He should be kept with them and taken for better training to be a good Muslim. His father had agreed, one less mouth to feed.

He had been sent into the desert to the training camps. Rafid had good food and was with his brothers. Everyone prayed, learned the Koran, and the most radical readers of the holy book preached to him and his comrades in arms on a daily basis. Soon, he understood the war his fellow soldiers were fighting, protecting their religion against the invading armies. All the world was attacking them, trying to stop the one true faith. It was easy, obvious in fact, the only thing really to do. Rafid went on to follow some of the most radical Islamist clerics, who showed him the way. Showed him the only way was to stop the march of terrorism against Islam and take the battle to the enemy and stop them. He had trained for many months, hoping he would be chosen for the most important task, to blow the Jews and the Christians to pieces, taking the war to them.

Rafid knew, as he had been promised by the clerics, that his parents would be so proud to have a true hero who died for the cause. Not many were chosen. Mom and Dad would be revered in the town, receiving money and gifts from the mosque and the people. He would be remembered forever as the man who went to Paradise.

They were close now to the turning for the Peponi Hotel. Rafid just hoped his pathetic partner Parvez would not let them down. He was sitting and sweating beside Rafid, moaning and crying about his family and life. Rafid had tried to help him, to pray with him, and show him the way to glory, but Parvez seemed to have lost his mind. He just sat and mumbled about being too young to die, he stank of piss too. Rafid would never let himself be seen like this.

Chapter Ten

The Pajero made a left turn onto the single lane, rough, dirt road heading towards the hotel. Everything was going according to plan so far. Rafid had a self-satisfied smile on his face. The agreed time to reach the hotel was 21:00, sharp. The dancing would be in full swing, the guests all occupied, watching the show.

The car lurched as it picked its way through the potholes. The sweat was pouring down his face, an early explosion would not be good! The road was unlit, with palm trees and a drainage ditch on either side to take the torrential rainwater away. It was as straight as an arrow, cut carefully with a grader. At the end, the hotel was a shining beacon of light, then the dark beach beyond. Taking his sweaty palm off the wheel, he checked his old Timex. It glowed red in the dark, 20:55, perfectly on time. His brothers would all be checking their watches about now, impatient to get on with the mission, waiting for his grand arrival.

Rafid was praying to himself, preparing his mind and body for Allah, singing praises to the one great God who would greet him with open arms in five short minutes.

Parvez sat beside him, shaking uncontrollably. There was no way out, nothing he could do, conned into this by his brother who had introduced him to Malik. now he was here, dying like a martyr. But he did not want to die. It was not his time, he had never even touched a woman let alone thought of children. Escape was all he could think of, the dark-haired stranger who had promised him, had let him down, deserted him. Parvez knew he was dead, his stomach gurgled again, the bile rose in his throat as he bent over, vomiting onto the floor of the car. Rafid looked at him in disgust.

Rafid saw a car skid almost broadside into the turning behind them. It came racing up the track, flashing its lights and blaring its horn, trying to overtake. Rafid was unconcerned. There were no passing places on this road, the fools would just have to wait. They would die in the blast anyway, two more to add to the death toll.

Parvez looked out the window at the car behind, swerving from side to side looking for a way past. He was shocked as the dark-haired stranger's head and body appeared out of the passenger's side door. He was waving his arms shouting for them to get out of the way. Rafid had also seen this and started speeding up.

Parvez's eyes were bulging out of his head, his lips contorted into a sick smile. The vomit was still stuck around his lips, mixing with the sweat running down his face. His greasy, unwashed hair plastering his scalp, he let out a crackled laugh.

Rafid looked at his accomplice with hate and disgust. This was no way to meet Allah.

Then Parvez spoke, "That is my savior behind us. He has come to stop you. You will not kill me!"

Rafid shouted, "What are you talking about?"

Parvez went on, "He came to me in the night in our prison in Kikambala. He made me tell him all about Abdi's plan, he promised to save me, now he is here. I will not die, I will live!"

Rafid immediately realized they had been betrayed from within. This was worse than cowardice. He slammed his foot on the accelerator. The car lurched forward, speeding up. The bomb would be early, but they had no choice, Parvez had messed with their perfect plan.

Rafid pulled the gun Abdi had given him and aimed it at Parvez, "You will die for your, treachery!"

Parvez smiled the smile of an addled brain, opened the door and jumped out, followed by a full magazine, seventeen shots all flying wide as Rafid attempted to keep control of the precious car bomb.

Parvez rolled out of the car, walloping the road. His light body bounced on the track like a plastic bottle thrown out of a moving car by a lazy tourist. It had been a thoughtless act of a broken mind to get away from the bullets. As his body smashed against the unforgiving surface of the road, it occurred to him the stranger would probably drive over his head and kill him anyway. But he did not care. All he wanted was out right now, how or where was not the problem. Even a prison cell was better than dead. Barry jammed on the brakes as he saw the figure fling itself out of the car. The Loner skidded to a halt, inches from Parvez's head. Brody leaped out of the vehicle, grabbed the prostrate, stinking, unconscious body and threw it onto the flatbed of the Landrover. He jumped back into the car as it sped off after the Pajero.

Rafid did not care that his weak partner had left, his mission was still on. The Landrover could not possibly stop him now. There was only about 1000 yards to go. The lights from the hotel were like a flashing beacon onshore, guiding him into safe harbor.

Brody stood up and emptied the Ithaca's five shots in the direction of the Pajero, knowing most would miss, but all he needed was one lucky shot to hit the bomb, the fuel tank, or a tire. He managed to blow the back window out with one of the blasts, but it must have missed the driver as the vehicle carried on towards its goal. This guy was on a mission. There was going to be only one way of stopping him, it had to be final.

Rafid felt the rear window of the Pajero explode into a thousand pieces, some hitting the back of his head and cutting his cheeks. Another shot hit the side mirror, another went through the back door, missing the petrol tanks by a hair then punching into the passenger seat. Rafid glanced in the rear-view mirror. A man was standing up on the seats of the Landrover with a pump-action shotgun, shooting at him! Then the Landrover slammed into the back of the Pajero as Barry tried to push it off the road. But the track was too narrow, the Loner could not get a good purchase on the rear wing. Rafid swerved on the perilously narrow track, one wheel went over the edge of the drainage ditch, he thought for a second his mission was over, but he managed to pull the car back onto the road and continue.

The two cars raced on into the night. Barry was still blasting his pitiful horn and flashing his lights, hoping to let the guests know this was not part of the show!

Rafid could clearly see his mission now. He could make out the guests dancing under the bright spotlights down in the foyer of the hotel. He would be joining them soon, and they could all depart this earth together. All he needed was to stay ahead of the Landrover. The blood from his cuts was running down his face. He looked like an avenging angel swooping in to clear the infidels from the world. Slamming the clutch down, he dropped a gear and raced for the Promised Land.

Barry looked down for a second as he fought the Loner to keep her on the road. The speedometer was bouncing from zero to eighty as they raced towards the hotel. He could see it had a wide, circular approach to the main entrance, with a huge foyer where the guests would be greeted, then further back a main reception and booking desk.

Brody shouted, "He'll try to get as far inside as possible to increase the amount of collateral damage."

Barry gritted his teeth and nodded, willing the Loner to just go that bit faster.

Rafid knew what to do. He had to turn right a little to line himself up with the flower bed in the center of the entrance, then take a straight line to the reception desk where most of the people were. He would drive straight through it, then detonate the bomb. The line of approach was not quite right, the road and the flower bed got in the way. It was a risk with the car behind him but one he would have to achieve to get into the reception. There was no other way.

Rafid was ready to die for his beliefs, he was on his journey to Paradise, he started chanting, "Allah Akbar, Allah Akbar," heading for the end.

The Pajero swerved to the right. Barry saw the turn and his chance! He hammered the poor Landrover forward. It was only a few feet behind the Pajero. The Landrover clipped the back right of the Pajero. The left-hand tire took the full weight of the vehicle as the right rear wheel lifted off the ground. Barry watched everything in slow motion. He saw himself raise the Redhawk up and out of the window, then he watched as his finger pulled the trigger. Later, when he was telling the story for the hundredth time, he swore he could see the .480 bullets leaving the end of the barrel. All six rounds were fired one after the other as fast as his finger could pull the trigger and the chamber could turn. Six flames of light, three bullets hit the rear right-hand tire, two stitched the back door, and one went through the front tire, bounced off the rim, then through the wing cowling and into the engine.

The Pajero was on its last legs, but it was still going. Rafid hauled the steering wheel to the left to counteract the impact on the rear right of the car, pulling the vehicle to correct it heading over the garden, but he was now too far to the right of the entrance.

After swerving and hitting the Pajero, the Landrover veered to the left. Barry had lost control when he was shooting the Pajero's tires out. The Loner leaped up the curb to the left-hand side of the flower garden and flew through the air, landing on two passenger-side wheels. It bounced onto its four tires, throwing the passengers around the cab like rag dolls. The Landrover then went straight through the service gate to the kitchen delivery area, skidding into a huge steel rubbish drum. The car stopped dead, throwing Barry against the 109's steering wheel, ripping a chunk out of his chin and taking two teeth. Brody headbutted the windscreen and was thrown back into his chair.

The Pajero careered on, bouncing off the first wooden pillar holding the roof of the hotel up, knocking the car off course again. Then it piled straight into the second post. The four by four was still traveling at about thirty miles an hour. It hit the thick tree trunk straight on. The front bumper buckled and the chassis twisted, pushing the engine back towards the driver. Rafid was thrown forward, smashing his head against the windscreen. He lay dazed for a second, then tried to move, but his legs were jammed between the seat and the steering column. He looked around. Suddenly everything was silent, all the noise, all the motion had stopped. Peering through the broken windscreen, he could hear shouts coming from inside the hotel. Rafid was ready. He knew this was the time. He had failed to get inside the hotel, but he was close enough the explosion would still do its primary job.

The young man from Lebanon sat in the smoldering wreckage of the car. Time was running out. In the last moments, he sat in contemplation, gripping the small silver necklace his father had presented to him with such serious honor all those months ago, back home. He could clearly see his mother crying. His sister looking at him with those lovely, innocent, almond eyes, not knowing what was going on. He saw his mosque back in Lebanon, then whispered goodbye. Rafid closed his eyes, said: "Allah Akbar" then pressed the small button strapped to his leg.

At that precise moment in time, Rafid ceased to exist. For an instant, he was a light, pink mist. As the fireball erupted the mist was evaporated all within a split second. The Semtex exploded, igniting the fuel. The explosion let loose hundreds of pounds of nails into the night. The nails coming out of the rear of the car flew for nearly two miles, before impaling themselves in palm trees or landing on the open scrubland. Kids would be picking them up for months and selling them in the market. The nails to the right flew towards the car park. The red-hot pieces of hardened steel, like rivets fresh from the furnace flying at supersonic speed, shredded the empty, smashing their windows. Two immediately exploded as their fuel tanks were pierced.

The blast to the right went across a flower garden, knocking over the wall and the gate to the service entrance. It then picked the Loner up and casually threw it on its side, pushing it towards the far wall. The nails came like hornets screaming in the dark, peppering the underside of the Landrover, making holes in the bottom footwells. The roof of the Pajero was blown straight up into the dried palm frond ceiling of the foyer. It immediately erupted in flame. The 'Makuti' was dry, catching like a wildfire on a hot, dry savannah, racing across the roof at two hundred miles an hour, destroying everything it touched.

The front blast went straight down towards the reception desk. The four security guards who were running to find out what had happened with the car were ripped to pieces, their bodies thrown like paper in the wind back towards the reception. When the fireball hit the employees welcoming the new arrivals, they disappeared.

The dancers were blown off their feet and over a wall. They were lucky the nails smashed into the wall a second later. The two receptionists and eight guests were blown off their feet, then hit with the fire and the nails. Their bodies were lacerated into pieces as if they had been attacked with a thousand razor blades.

Brody slowly opened his eyes. He had been knocked unconscious as the car was thrown over and against the wall. Barry was next to him, groaning. His face covered in blood, his nose was twisted at a strange angle. Brody checked himself. His arm was swelling up, he had cuts on his face and hands but was still in action. He kicked the windscreen out of the Landrover, then dragged Barry out onto the scorched concrete covered in nails. Barry was gradually recovering. A flap of skin was hanging off below his chin, bleeding steadily, his shirt was changing color, but he could stand.

Brody said, "Barry are you OK?"

"Me, mate, I'll survive. Not sure about the Loner, though, she looks fucked!"

Brody went on, "Can you help? There must be pandemonium going on in there. I need to get to the beach to stop this."

Barry glanced around, "What about the kid we picked, where's he at?"

They ran around the courtyard, looking for Parvez, he was in a pile of kitchen waste his clothes were smoldering, but he was alive. Barry grabbed him, tied him quickly to a pole, and gave him a left hook for good luck, Parvez slumped down, unconscious again.

Brody reached for his Glock and raced off towards the kitchen.

He came out into the dining area about halfway towards the beach. There were gunshots all around, but mostly from the shoreline.

Malik had heard the explosion and immediately got to his feet. It was no surprise, he had been impatiently waiting for several hours! He did not know how well it had gone, his station was deep inside the hotel. Pulling the AK47 from a large green bush, he started his work. The first order was to shoot a pretty young wife, her husband, and two kids as they rushed past trying to get away from the fire. Then he shot into the air to cause panic, pushing the guests towards the beach. The other four were doing the same. If the tourists did not run or obey, instantly they were shot where they stood. Men, women, children, it did not matter they were just dirty Jews.

Malik was pushing the crowd forward. Reaching the top of the beach, he could see the four boats at the water's edge waiting for the hostages.

The Somalis were already loading people onto the boats in the shallows. The guests did not know if this was a rescue or what, they were just following in panic and shock, like sheep to the slaughter.

Brody came out of the long dining hall and watched as the people were herded forwards. Dodging to the right behind a wall, then jumping through a bush, he landed in the garden beside the beach. One of Malik's men was ten feet away from him, pointing his weapon at a family cowering behind some sunbeds. Brody walked up behind him, As he got close, he shot him in the liver. The guy did not know what had just happened, he did not realize he was dead yet. His body and brain refused to understand that it was all over. An instant later he collapsed onto the grass.

Brody said, "Run to the side. Do not go to the beach! Go left or right but not to the beach and not to the reception!"

He took the Ak47 off the dead terrorist and jogged forward. He did not know how many Somalis there were, but out of the six Palestinians, there were only three now, much better odds. His short-term plan was to cause more panic, shoot into the air scaring the guests along the beach, away from the fire and boats. Brody reached the sand and saw about one hundred people milling around at the water's edge. One boat was already loaded and being pushed off the beach. The other three were still collecting their cargo of unknowing hostages.

Malik watched as Brody came over the small rise and onto the beach, he aimed carefully and shot the newcomer carrying the gun. Brody was sent sprawling on his back as a sharp pain shot through his upper shoulder. He instinctively rolled for cover into a dip on the beach, then carefully explored his shoulder to see the damage. There was a small entry wound and a larger one on his back, a through and through it was painful but not life-threatening yet. He had to be more careful. Wiggling to the top of the sand dune, he peered into the darkness. Malik had disappeared among the crowd of hostages in the shallows

Brody rolled into the depression, got to his feet, and ran down, using the shadows to get closer to the Somalis loading the three remaining vessels.

The first speed boat to leave had lowered its outboard halfway and started the engine. It was currently pushing through the shallows towards deeper water. When it reached the six-foot-deep mark, the captain pressed the trim tilt button to lower the engine fully into the water. They could then head the ten miles out to sea with the hostages and load them onto the mother ship. There was another guard in the bow with his back to the ocean, pointing his weapon at their guests.

The captain did not see or hear *Shukran* appear out of the darkness. Gumbao was on the port rail holding his AK47 up to his shoulder. The dhow immediately veered off to starboard as the speed boat came to midships. Gumbao let loose a volley. It went through the captain of the boat and into the engine. The boat died. It was finished with no power, there was nothing to be done. The guard spun around to see the stern of *Shukran* disappearing into the gloom, he was helpless, dead in the water.

Brody moved closer to the crowd. There was a dull ache in his arm and blood was dripping from his finger-tips. The second Palestinian was just a few feet ahead and to the left near the water. He moved silently and stealthily behind him. The guy was mixed in with the innocent tourists, all close together. It would be dangerous, the terrorists could just open fire. Brody was about to grab the guy but stopped. There was gunfire out on the water. He looked out to see a mirage almost invisible in the dark. *Shukran* came into view, with Gumbao standing on the gunwale, holding the AK. He looked like a vengeful Viking appearing from the dark, raking the rear of the first speed boat then disappearing again.

This panicked the terrorists. Brody took his chance in the melee, grabbed the second guy by the throat, pulling it long, stretching the neck as far as it would go, separating the vertebrae just enough. The man's feet were leaving the ground, then with a quick, practiced action, he twisted first left then right. The limp body fell to his feet in the shallow water, without a sound.

The second boat was full. A Palestinian and a Somali were pushing it off the beach. The Somali jumped into the vessel, the Palestinian pushed a little further, up to his knees in the water, and was about to leap onto the side when he stopped. Brody watched as the back of his head exploded. The Somali captain put the AK47 down on the back seat and shouted to the guard to keep the people quiet.

Malik watched as his own man was shot by the captain, instantly realizing they had been betrayed. He ran over to the next boat, signaling his last man to follow him. He pushed through the crowd, shoving the guests out of the way, not caring about hostages anymore. This was survival, escape was all that was left. He screamed at the Somali Captain, "Ya akho el sharmouta!" 'You brother of a whore.' They had screwed them over. He dragged the Somali captain off his boat and threw him in the water double tapping him in the chest for good measure. The guard who was manhandling the hostages jumped up, swinging his weapon up to bear. But Malik was quicker, cutting him in half with a long burst from his machine gun, sweeping right through his torso. Two guests also went down, falling into the water.

The area was in total pandemonium. Malik jumped on the boat and his last remaining comrade pushed the boat back into deeper water.

The second boat was doing the same as the first, moving with the engine half tilted until they reached deeper water. When they hit the six-foot mark, the captain lowered the engine, rammed into gear, and started heading for the open ocean. Hassan was sitting on *Shukran*, just off the beach about forty yards past the small surf line. He watched the radar as the second boat got into deeper water and started moving forward, adjusting their course to come just ahead of them, where they would speed up. The vessel showed up as a dark green, flashing blob on the red radar screen. The speed boat was moving out into the swells. The captain knew he had only ten miles in a straight line to get his valuable cargo back to the mother ship. The longer ocean waves started to lift and drop the boat. He was ready to push the throttle handles to full. The two 150HP engines would scream into life throwing the craft through the water at forty knots.

Then he sensed as much as saw *Shukran* appear on the port side. The nose came out of the dark. It smashed into the forward port side of the light speed boat. *Shukran* was made of solid hardwood from ancient trees, like a floating battering ram. The bow stove-in the sidewall of the fiberglass boat then continued through the front of the speed boat, tearing through the floor and straight through the starboard sidewall. Suddenly the bow was missing from the craft, but the engines were still pushing. She immediately filled with water. The Somali captain started shouting. The guard raised his weapon and fired some shots off at the side of *Shukran*, but it was useless. The planks absorbed the bullets hardly noticing them. Gumbao popped his head up, shooting over their heads. The captain and the guard both knew they were finished and threw their weapons overboard. The speed boat was sinking fast. Hassan rammed *Shukran* into reverse. The collision had slowed her. The engine pulled her back through the water. As the guests swam towards the wooden boat. Hassan placed the old rusty dive ladder over the side, the guests climbed aboard gratefully, the captain and his guard last. The barrel of Gumbao's AK pointed at their centers of mass as Hassan tied them to *Shukran's* thick, wooden mast, then handed one of the newcomers a Glock and said, "Those guys move, you shoot them."

Shukran came about and headed off, looking for the first boat to rescue the passengers. Hassan had marked it on the radar so they could trackback to it easily in the darkness.

Brody saw Malik shoot the two Somalis. He realized that there was more than one plan working here. The Palestinians were going to be used as scapegoats. Brody slipped the Glock into the back of his jeans, then pushed through the thinning crowd milling around on the beach. Everyone was panicking, they did not know what to do. The guests had thought they were being saved with these boats. Then the people on the boats had started shooting. They were now moving en-masse back towards the hotel, which was crackling, the flames reaching thirty feet into the air. The palm frond roof had burnt like a bush fire. The whole place was ablaze. It would be seen for miles. This confused the guests further. They could not go to the beach or the hotel, so sort of hung around screaming and crying in the no man's land between the two. Everyone was in shock, their brains numbed by all the violence and death around them. All they could think of was safety in numbers.

Brody came up to the bow of the last boat on the beach. He simply walked up and shot the guard through the back of the head. He was in a hurry and had no time for messing about with prisoners. He threw himself onto the boat. The captain turned around, holding his machine gun, aiming poorly, he let off a couple of wide shots. It gave Brody enough time. He rolled across the deck, came up on his knee, and put one through the captains' chest, then one through his nose and the last through the top of his skull. The man fell to the side, the impact from the Glock rounds pushing him over the gunwale. The dead body splashed heavily into the water and lay face down with a dark shadow blooming around him.

Brody could see Malik was reversing away from the beach. He dipped the outboard as far as he dared, not wanting it to hit the sand, then pulsed the engine, revving it and letting it pause, pulling the boat off the beach. The bow was still sliding on the bottom. Brody revved the engine again and again slowly loosening it from the suction of the sand, at the same time creating a massive rooster's tail behind the boat. Taking a chance, he gave it full reverse. A plume of white water shot up into the air, as the engine roared sucking water, air, and sand into the cooling system. The speed boat slid back into the sea.

Malik was already heading out towards the ocean, he had a good fifty yards' head start. Brody swung the wheel to the left, then rammed the boat into forward gear. The engine complained. It was not fully submerged and was sucking more air than the cooling water it needed. The tortured engine pushed the speed boat away towards the ocean. As soon as Brody dared, he lowered the outboard bit by bit. The gearbox hit a small sandbar. Brody lifted the engine slightly to allow them to pass, then immediately dropped it again. As they reached deeper water, he had closed the gap to about twenty-five yards. Brody dropped both outboards completely and felt the powerful engines push the speed boat ahead with a surge.

Malik was doing the same. He was racing off into the night. Brody had to keep site of him or he would be lost along the coast. Brody felt the boat beneath him. During his years in the special boat service, he had driven every kind of off and inshore boat you could imagine. Finally, he was in his area of expertise. He knew he could catch the last Palestinian, and finish this.

Chapter Eleven

Brody was trailing Malik but making headway. Malik could drive a boat but had nowhere near the skills the Special Boat Service training and years of combat had given him. The two vessels were racing directly out to sea. As the waves grew longer, the craft could increase speed even more, until both throttles were at their stops, flying through the water fully on the plane, only the engines' gearboxes submerged in the darkness of the night.

Brody had a major problem. He needed to stop the other boat. All he had was his Glock. He also had a hole in his shoulder. Driving and shooting were out of the question. His throbbing arm was hanging loosely by his side, the blood was still pouring out of the wound, dripping off the end of his fingers onto the fiberglass deck, only to be washed away instantly. His legs were feeling unsteady. A wave of tiredness washed over him. If he just slowed down and had a rest he could carry on. He shook himself awake, with renewed determination. The last few weeks had been a nightmare, now he was about to finish it. Don't think, just do!

With renewed energy to get the job done, Brody had to give a final push then he could rest. He was sitting in the wake of the lead vessel, allowing it to break the surface tension of the waves, creating a bed of bubbles with less friction running against the hull of his craft. He was getting close now, a bit too close. Malik's last soldier started emptying his AK47 clip into the bow. The two boats were leaping out of the water as they crested waves, bouncing through the air. Only a few rounds clipped the bow, but all it took was one lucky shot.

Malik started taking a long, wide turn, probably thinking of heading up the coast to find an inlet where they could lay low before heading back out of the country. Brody saw his chance. It was full of risk but he was past caring. He needed to stop the other boat. Planning and safety had long since gone out of the window. He swung out of the wake, heading straight across the arc the other vessel was making. The soldier standing at the stern of the lead boat was staring into the pitch darkness of the ocean behind him. The chase boat had been there a couple of seconds ago, just before he let loose a whole magazine of Soviet 7.62 rounds in his direction. He smiled, one or two shots must have made their mark. Either the other guy was dead or his boat had been disabled. He reached forward with his free hand and tapped Malik on the shoulder, pointing behind them. Malik smiled. At last, they would get free, then make their way back to Wajir and home. He would make a full report to his father, then start the revenge attack on Muna and Abdi, their families would die first with photographic evidence, maybe a few body parts through special delivery. Then friends, pets, and anyone else they could lay their hands on. Malik knew his father, he would not take this lightly.

The boat came out of the darkness, flying off the top of a swell straight into Malik's speeding vessel. Brody hit the fiberglass hull just forward of midships. The bottom of the flying boat slid over the gunwale of the racing craft. Brody's engine screamed as it left the water. Malik tried to turn away to shake off the spinning propeller, but Brody was traveling too fast. The boat slid over the top hull against the gunwale, skating across and down towards the center console. The engine was still revving at five thousand revolutions per minute, but the prop was out of the water, screaming. The stern of the top craft raced along the top of the gunwales of the lower boat, the spinning propeller smashing into the center console, ripping into Malik's arms, tearing huge chunks of flesh off his body, chewing into his jaw then up through his face. The splintering center console was torn apart, Malik was thrown back onto his engines and flipped over the side into the ocean. Brody's boat was tossed over the side of the lower craft. The engine spun the boat into the water on the port side. As this was all happening, in a last-ditch effort for survival, Brody threw himself over the starboard side of his boat, landing in a bleeding heap in the bows of the vessel below.

The out of control flying craft careened off the port side, flipping itself as it hit the water, landing next to them half submerged. Both engines died almost at once. Brody's vessel sank immediately. He was left sitting in a disabled craft with a terrified soldier trying to stay as far away as possible from the blood-covered lunatic who had just arrived out of nowhere. There was loud thrashing in the water behind them. The bull sharks were happy at least!

They sat in silence for what seemed like an age. Brody was wondering how the hell he was going to get out of this one. It seemed pointless to try really. Just close his eyes and rest, that was the best option. The waves of sleep came crashing over him. The blood was leaving much faster than it could be replaced. There were only nine pints, to begin with, about nine beers. Not such a lot. He dreamed of swimming to the shore, but the sharks followed his fat blood trail, jerking awake as they lunged at his legs in the water. Finally, it was hopeless, you cannot fight the end. His vision was gone, or it was too dark to see. The water was washing around his waist in the sinking boat. What the hell. It didn't matter now anyway; might as well let it all happen. He slipped gratefully into unconsciousness.

He did not feel or see Gumbao jump off *Shukran* and land lightly beside him. The tough old seaman dragged the unconscious body to its feet. Then gently lifted it onto his tough broad shoulders and climbed back up the rusty old ladder to *Shukran*. Hassan had become a real genius on the radar, tracking the two boats all the way through their chase, guessing where they would end up then heading for that point. Gumbao carefully put Brody on the rear bench seat, then wrapped his wound as the dhow, full of Israeli refugees and several captives, headed back to Mtwappa Creek.

The four-by-four drove along the broken tracks, then through the streams and later small rivers leading to the exact location Abdi had given them. The hand-held GPS glowed in the dark, pointing them this way and that. Sometimes their route was blocked by trees or a large muddy sandbank. But all in all the small team made good progress. The soldiers reached the exact spot a little early, giving them plenty of time to set up. Mallaba sat on the roof of the car, his buddies wandering around smoking and chatting. In the distance, there was a bright orange glow. The group laughed at the fire and explosion. Tonight would go down in history. When they got home, they would be heroes: a new wife each and roasted goat for a month.

At the allotted time, the Boeing 757 lumbered along the runway and dragged its 220,000 pounds gradually up into the night sky. Mallaba watched the plane through the target locator of the Strela launcher counting the seconds watching the image grow in front of him. At the last second, as the aircraft banked to head off towards Tel Aviv, he pressed the fire button on the Strela missile control board. The launch almost threw him off the top of the car. The heat-seeking rocket flew off into the night. It wobbled in the sky for a second then locked onto its target. The soldiers watched in awe. This was going to be something big for sure. The rocket raced off towards the plane. It would take less than five seconds to reach the port engine and destroy it, probably taking the wing off as well. All 239 Jewish passengers plus flight crew would die in a horrible fireball. The Al-Shabaab could not believe it. The plane suddenly started firing fireworks and shiny string out of the back. It came in a huge shower, like the Fourth of July, loads of bright flashes and silver tape shooting into the air in all directions, floating behind the plane. Then a larger object shot out the back of a hatch. It was like a glowing sun flying through the air. The Strela missile decided this was a much better target and went straight for it. Exploding in the air, missing the jet by at least five hundred yards. Mallaba reached for a second missile. This time he would not fail. Then around him, a flock of small birds started flying. But his men collapsed as the sound of tiny birds or moths racing through the air filled his ears. He looked down. His body was suddenly turning red as the pain crept up through his chest. The last thing he saw was the car below him, the windows smashing, and holes appearing on all sides.

Colonel Rabi had received the call from Barry. At first, he thought it was more ghosts in the smoke. But after making inquiries about the hotel and discovering it was full of Israelis, he felt prudence was the best course of action. First, he notified the airline of the potential of a missile strike as they took off. Strangely, they thanked him and said it was all OK nothing could hit the plane. Then he dispatched his training team on a special exercise at the end of Mtwappa Creek. Supposedly an insurgency group had entered and were threatening the airport. The Kenyan troops were overjoyed at sneaking around in the forest on a night exercise. Colonel Rabi gave them the full kit, night vision, and infrared scanners. Looking at the map, there were only a couple of places a missile could be fired. The exercise was set in this general location. And as a last-minute thought, to ensure the trainees treated the fun and games a bit seriously, everyone was given live ammunition. If Major William Brody was a crackpot as he suspected, his ass was covered. If not, his guys would come across the threat. He knew with the firepower and excitement the trainees had, no one stood a chance in fact. A couple of his guys would probably come back wounded.

Epilogue

A faint light glimmered, almost annoying as it moved erratically up and down, left to right, sometimes slowly, sometimes quickly. It flashed, and blinked, alternating, even the colors changed. Then a noise in the background, you had to strain your ears to hear it. Quietly repeating itself. He listened, then thought, *"Really. Was it all worth the trouble."* The place was warm, almost womb-like, comfortable. No need to hurry. Then the bloody light again, up down, left right, flashing, this was a crap dream. No fun at all. The noise was increasing, getting louder. Brody, William Brody, Major William Brody. His name, why was someone calling his name from the womb? Finally, he cracked an eyelid. It hurt like a needle was being shoved straight through his eyeball, so he closed it again, slumping back into a dream world.

The next thing was hunger. His stomach was growling like a caged animal. He could not remember when he had eaten last. It must have been ages ago before he slept. The hunger pangs had a long argument with his eyes but the hunger won. They opened one at a time, slowly. The pain didn't return, the flashing lights were gone. Two wonderful smiles greeted him, Wanjiku and Emaculata had taken turns sitting by the bed in Mombasa hospital. His wound was not serious, but the blood loss had taken three days of a coma to get itself back in line and allow his body to start functioning again.

After some food and another day, he was released on light duties back to *Shukran*. His shoulder hurt like hell, his head was cut and bruised, but nothing life-threatening. He winced as he stepped out of the hospital into the bright sunlight of a new day, five days after the explosion in Kikambala. Wanjiku had a car waiting which took him straight to the Full Moon Bar. Barry was there with a cold one in his hand, a big white bandage on his chin, and a smaller one across his nose. Both of his eyes were still a deep purple.

"Gooday, mate, what's up? You look like shit. I wish all nurses looked like that. Not sure the skirt is all that practical in a working environment!" He said with a big smile.

Brody sat gingerly on a stool, holding his beer, "Barry that was one hell of a trip. I left you at the hotel then I don't remember anything."

Barry took a swig from his glass, then went on, "Mate, I did fine. Bloody cars a wreck, completely fucked it is. But I don't care, plenty more where that came from. The army dressed like civilians have been looking for you, I am sure they will be along soon."

Brody took a long pull on his beer, "So what's the story? What happened?"

Barry was very happy to fill in the blanks, "Mate, you are a bloody hero. You saved the day. After you ran off to get the bad guys, I went and helped. That bloody bomb was bad. I just jumped in and did what I could, used my first aid skills. The army and police soon turned up. I showed them the guy we slapped, and they took him away. Then I helped the people as best as I could. The Israelis turned up double quick and closed the place down. They asked me a bunch of questions, then I was allowed to go home. The Army even dropped me off right on me doorstep."

They chatted for a while as Wanjiku fussed over him, making him eat loads of healthy roasted meat. Barry offered him a room at the back for a couple of days. *Shukran* was not the best place for recuperation.

Later in the week, Brody sat at one of the tables overlooking the creek feeling much better. Gumbao and Hassan had recounted their stories about the attack and rescuing Brody from the speed boat. They had then towed it back to the creek behind the dhow. Gumbao seemed to have claimed some sort of International Salvage Rights over it. Anyone who was foolish enough to argue saw a side of Gumbao that was not so nice. He had a gun now as well, taken from one of the Al-Shabab soldiers they had tied up and handed over to the soldiers. Brody made a mental note to remove it as soon as he could. The speed boat had been pretty badly beaten. But a fiberglass fundi had arrived and a mechanic. Work was currently underway. They were slowly building a flotilla, which was not such a bad thing. The boat was ideal for fishing and diving.

Barry was still feeling the pain of the Loner. Although he said it was not an issue, Brody could see it was. Something would have to be sorted out, another dip into the diamond fund.

One lunchtime, a shadow fell across the floor next to Brody. Colonel Rabi and another man were standing next to the table trying not to look like soldiers. Both dressed in blue jeans, sneakers, and button-down shirts.

He started with, "Major Brody, it is good to see you up and around. How is the wound?"

Brody looked at him with a smile, "It's fine, getting better every day. I'll be running again soon. Please sit, have a beer."

The two nonmilitary, military guys sat uncomfortably at the table. Brody ordered them beers just for the fun of it.

When they were sat suitably, embarrassed Brody asked, "So who's you friend Colonel Rabi?"

Rabi said, "Let me explain first. After our fantastic success at thwarting this terrorist attack on the Israelis and the Kenyans, we have forged even stronger links with the Kenyan Government. We caught one of the perpetrators a Parvez who is now in custody in our secure barracks in the port facility. We also stopped, as you may know, the attack on a civilian airline using a combined Mossad, Kenyan task force which proved very successful. After a vicious firefight, we suffered only two casualties. Unfortunately, all the Al-Shabab were killed in the action. Your assistance as our civilian contractor providing intel on the attacks was very useful. We were able to put forces on the ground, rescue the guests from the hotel and stop the attack." He finished with a sheepish grin on his face.

Brody said as he drank his beer, "That sounds about right to me."

The Colonel went on, "We informed the Kenyan Government about two fugitives probably heading north: one Abdi Mohammed Mahmoud and his partner a Muna Swaleh. They were stopped heading for Wajir. The driver died in the incident from over thirty bullet wounds, the other two are in Shimo-La-Tewa now, assisting the Kenyans with their enquiries."

Rabi breathed a noticeable sigh of relief and went on, "This is Lieutenant Colonel John Briggs from the UK. We work together on occasion and have been through your M.O.D. file. I must say it is impressive, I underestimated you when we first met."

The Lieutenant took over, "Major, after your fantastic work here helping Colonel Rabi sort out his mess, we have come up with a plan which we hope you would take a look at. This coast is open, there is no other word for it, just a bloody sieve really. Any and all points of entry are open to whatever, as I am sure you have realized. We would like some eyes and ears wandering around. You just keep doing what you are doing and when you see something, you give us a call. No need to get involved, just another set of eyes to help us, what do you think?"

Brody answered after a few seconds. "Not really my thing, if you would like to make a better offer. Like salaries for my guys and a new Landrover for Barry over there. You must know his was kind of blown up by a terrorist. He's a very chatty chap when he has had a few I can tell you, probably blurt everything out."

There were a few seconds of silence, then the two nonmilitary, military guys nodded. Rabi went on, "We thought you would say as much. It can be arranged. We will pay your two guys as Privates First Class in the British Army. You can assume the rank of Major again at full pay. We will provide you with a sat nav. telephone and some numbers, we will also call on you from time to time, asking you to have a holiday in a particular area where you might see something of interest. Oh, and I have a Landrover I need stored for a while safely, maybe you know where I can keep it!"

Brody laughed out loud. The British always convoluted, never actually straight, but he agreed, it was what he was doing anyway, so what the hell. The guys would be very happy they now had salaries. Hassan, he was sure, would send all of his home. His sister could head off to University in Dar-Es-Salaam. Brody would hold onto Gumbao's money. The guy did not even own two sets of clothing so a passport or ID and a bank account would be well out of the question. With that the diamonds, and the new boat, they were set for an easy time, diving, fishing and sailing. brilliant. What could possibly go wrong? Living the Dream......!

The End....

Dear Reader,

I sincerely hope you enjoyed this story as much as I have enjoyed writing it. The East African Coast has been my home now for nearly twenty years, and I love it as much as Brody does. All the locations are based on actual places and islands;

they can easily be found on Google Earth. The people in the story are fictitious, but they are based on people I know and have met over the years.

If you did enjoy the read, or in fact, if you didn't, I would very much appreciate some feedback on the book page. Just type in the title on Amazon Kindle and let me know what you think. Good or bad, I am always interested as the reviews make me a better writer for the future. I would also appreciate it if you could put me on Twitter or any other book sites where you think readers would enjoy this story.

Alternatively, my email is stevefreelancewriter@gmail.com I would love to hear from you, and I answer all of the emails personally.

I am now sat with Brody as he gets ready for his next tropical adventure. I am sure if you enjoyed this book, the third in the series, you will enjoy the next one, Where Brody battles with ivory smugglers from the Tsavo Game Park through the Tana River Delta and into the Indian Ocean. I am getting to know Brody as a character and his thought process, so the stories become more involved and I hope more enjoyable for you. This series will go on as long as he has interesting stories to tell.

I consider myself very lucky to have lived in East Africa for so long. I have traveled up and down this coastline fishing, diving, and exploring. Most of the descriptions are based on my actual experiences here. This, I think, puts me in a unique position to be able to give you the best and most realistic view on life in East Africa.

If you join William Brody's Newsletter using the link below or visiting the website, then I will let you know as soon as another installment is imminent.

If you would like to sign up for our Newsletter, then please click on this link and it will take you to our sign-up page. We don't send out loads of emails, just important stuff like book launches. We also keep your address personal to us. http://eepurl.com/ceoCSv We also have a website which you can visit if you would like at http://stevefreelancewriter.wordpress.com

Yours

Steve Braker

William Brody Action Adventure Series

Book Previews

This is the Third in the William Brody Series. I truly hope you are enjoyed the read. The other books are available through Amazon:

Book 1.   African Slaver

Just go to my web site and follow the links to your Amazon paperback page https://stevebrakerbooks.com/african-slaver/

Preview of African Slaver:

Chapter One

Sitting perfectly still, totally relaxed, suspended in space, Brody was 50 feet down, according to the depth gauge strapped to his arm, in crystal clear water, sitting motionless, and waiting. His Rolex Submariner was counting off the seconds; so far one hundred and twenty had slowly ticked past. Freediving is all about relaxing. You stop thinking, sitting in a trance like state, a Buddha hanging serenely in the ocean, holding a six-foot pole with a razor-sharp spear!

His lungs were relaxed and full. Life was all around him in the depths, constant movement and color from every direction. The current was very slightly pushing him to the northeast. His body felt warm even at this depth. He glanced up to monitor his position. Clearly visible above, the small wooden sailing craft was safely anchored to the reef. Earlier he had slipped off the boat, swimming until the bottom disappeared into nothingness. Then, after taking several deep breaths, he duck-dived, finning for a few strokes until the lead weights around his waist started slowly pulling him down.

Hassan was sat on the boat, fiddling with the engine nervously, tidying the ropes and sails, continuously glancing at the place where his new customer had just disappeared. The odd couple had met on the jetty a few days earlier. Hassan had spotted this new 'Muzungu,' a white guy, jumping off the weekly ferry. Hassan approached, with his best tourist grin plastered across his face, and offered to help the newcomer with the dive tanks and other equipment. As usual, this quickly flourished into finding accommodation, and a bite to eat. Hassan usually earned his daily cash catching fish, but Brody had come to dive. The two shook on an agreement. Brody would hire him, and his dhow with the small rusty outboard, on a daily basis until he left the island. This would also give Hassan a regular stable income for his mother, father, and sister, plus himself. The deal sat well with Hassan. It was guaranteed money, a rare thing on the island. He figured he could also do some fishing while his new customer was down below.

Brody's watch was still ticking away the seconds. He had about a minute left. He loved it down here. So silent and peaceful, away from the dreams and memories he fought against daily. His lungs started to tighten. He looked up again to the bottom of the boat; it seemed to be getting further away with every second ticking by, but Brody always wanted to push that little bit more, always one more step. He held on, then took careful aim. The lovely coley coley was swimming in circles about twenty feet away from him, interested in this motionless creature just sitting, not swimming, not moving, not breathing. Brody aimed and fired. The bolt from the spear gun was dead on target, just behind the pectoral fin. It went straight through the fish's heart. Brody's practiced aim was proving to be unstoppable here. But the water was crystal clear, he could easily see the bottom another sixty feet below him.

The fish was about 12 pounds, a good size. There were a ton of them living off this reef; this one would not be noticed. Brody believed in freediving for fish as it seemed fairer than using his tanks. At least the fish had some advantages over him in this alien environment.

The coley coley struggled, then went limp. They were known for being the least energetic of the large eating reef fish in tropical oceans. Brody quickly dragged it in, then started for the dhow above.

When his head broke the surface, it was still only 07:00, but the temperature was already nearly 100 degrees. He felt the tropical sun burning his scalp immediately. Paddling to stay afloat, Brody threw the line to Hassan, who gratefully took it and started hauling in the dead fish before the sharks got a scent of it.

Hassan shouted, "Hey, Boss, that was long. I thought you had joined the fish and swam away!"

Hassan always hid his fear that his boss and paymaster would disappear over the side and never come back!

He was a Swahili, the coastal tribe of East Africa, born in the water. They were natural boatmen, and could tell the weather, the wind, and tides before they could walk. They knew the best reefs, fishing spots, mooring points, and the finest of what the tiny town had to offer, which wasn't a great deal!

During their initial meeting, Hassan had taken Brody to a lovely secluded house, or shack depending on the way you looked. It was on an isolated beach and very quiet, with just the wind in the palms, and the waves lapping on the pale white shore. There were no luxuries like electricity. The water came from a well, dug some eighty feet further up the beach, away from the high tide line. The fishing hut was suspended above the water on stilts. The one-room, plus cubicle shower outback, was constructed of cut lengths of bamboo, tied together using twine weaved from coconut leaves. Hung just outside the rickety front door was an ancient, smoke-stained hurricane lamp, and inside was a small cot with a mosquito net slung above. That was about it for amenities. Hassan was not sure if it was what his new customer would like, but he had taken it without a second glance.

Brody did four more dives for fish that morning. He had only wanted one, but knew Hassan would be able to sell them in the market. His family would eat well tonight. Brody also knew the Swahilis were so generous he would get more food than he could eat, cooked by Hassan's mother, so the sentiment was not entirely altruistic.

After the last dive, Hassan coaxed the outboard back into life, which took a while. Brody pulled the big stone anchor off the bottom, and they set off back across the lagoon.

Brody sat on the small wooden deck of the boat, gutting the fish as they slowly headed back towards the village and his new shack. The journey would take about an hour as the outboard had seen much better days, and Hassan was praying over it to last until they reached home. He had gutted so many fish it was second nature; his mind started to wander. He was so lucky to have found this place, a tranquil paradise in the middle of nowhere; he could live peacefully and forget the past he so wanted to lose.

William Brody was born in the UK, in North London on the estates near Wood Green. The place was good enough, an average inner-city suburb, with a large shopping centre or mall to hang out in, and a public school, doctor's office and post office, all the usual stuff. His mother and father both wanted the best for him. His dad worked for the local council, and his mom in an insurance office on the high street. Life was all right, a bit mundane, but OK. Brody enjoyed school, but was not so good at the education part. Sports, especially swimming, was great, but sitting in the classroom was not so much fun. His reports always said that he could do better and must try harder. The inner cities didn't have a lot to offer Brody. Inheriting his father's wild Irish ways, he longed for the outdoors. When the school offered outdoor pursuits or camping, his name was at the top of the list. Every Friday, he would load his bike with camping gear and set off into the evening, not returning until late Sunday night.

Whenever school was too much, he would head down to Canary Wharf on the River Thames and watch the boats go by, smelling the tidal river as it raced in and out. His dream was to join the Merchant or the Royal Navy and sail the seas for the rest of his life; he could think of no better way to spend his days, afloat on the water he loved so much.

On his sixteenth birthday, he applied for the Merchant Navy, but was turned down as his grades in school were frankly rubbish, plus the few scrapes with the law did not help. The next stop was the Royal Navy. The recruiting officer acted the same way.

The Sargent said, "Look, lad, you can go and do better at these exams and come back after a couple of years."

Brody was not happy. He asked out of exasperation, "What else is there?"

The recruiting Sargent looked him up and down, then said, "Well, lad, you look damn fit. What about the Royal Marines?"

He had not thought about them before. It would be at least near or on boats. One second later, the forms were signed, his dad breathed a deep sigh of relief and handed the lad over to the Royal Marines.

With a jolt, Brody was back to the small fishing boat. All the fish had been gutted and were laying at his feet. The boat was only a few minutes from the small jetty. Hassan expertly maneuvered the dhow up against the wooden poles. They landed the five coley coley on the quay, and Hassan immediately found a basket made from coconut fronds. they seemed to use them for everything. He then raced off along the dusty track towards the small fish market. Brody knew Hassan would get a good price for the fresh fish because the local boats had not left before 04:00 this morning, and it was a good eight hours' round trip.

Hassan met his sister along the track, and gave one of the fish to take home to their mother for the feast tonight. Since Brody had landed on the island, the family's fortunes had changed. They were starting to enjoy his company, and the rent from the little house on the beach also helped.

Brody collected his gear and headed off down the beach towards his pad. It would be noon soon. This place would touch 100 degrees Fahrenheit, combined with ninety-five percent humidity. No fans or air conditioning made the situation almost unbearable. His usual pastime during the baking afternoons was to find some shade and slump in a hammock or wander the beach looking for interesting shells. Often, he would meet some local fishermen, sitting on the beach mending nets. Chatting with them was enjoyable. The old men did not have a word of English nor him Swahili, but they were good-natured and happy to have someone with new stories to tell. In the way of travellers meeting for the first time, after a while, and using many hand signals and drawing pictures in the wet sand, everything became clear.

The Marines, then the Special Boat Service had instilled in him the importance of learning the language and culture. Mixing with the locals was second nature. Brody sat and patiently learned one word after the other. Earlier in the week, the old men had taught him 'Samaki,' the Swahili word for fish. He was going to use is a new word tonight at the meal.

Right now, all he wanted to do was head back to the little house and take a snooze. Freediving was always tiring. The dull ache inside his head was growing as he wandered back along the soft white sands of the beach to the shack.

Although this was a strictly Muslim island, the elders always managed to find a local drink called 'Mnazi' made from fermented coconut juice. When he got to the shack, two old men were sitting on the porch. They had gnarled fingers and hands like tree bark. Once they had been fishermen, but were too old for that hard life now. The two old men spent their days mending nets, sharpening hooks, and telling stories about when the fish were bigger and the ocean was more terrible. They also liked to sneak a drink. With three wives each and who knew how many children, who could blame them! These old reprobates had snuck off and decided Brody's house was a good idea. The plan was to blame the 'Muzungu,' white man, if they got caught.

The 'Mnazi' was sweet like treacle. The old men had three small wooden cups with short hollow sticks for straws poking out of the top. The bottom of the straw had old sailcloth wrapped around the base as a filter. 'Mnazi' came in ancient, battered gourds and was reverently poured equally into each cup. Pieces of coconut husk floated on top of the milky drink. It did not smell so good either, but it was potent. The trick was to hold your nose for the first couple of shots, then the smell seemed to disappear.

The fishermen had a good haul. Brody knew he would drink too much.

Get this book or any one of the other three in the series. Happy reading!

Steve Braker.

Join my mailing list, so I can let you know when more books are available. Just head to https://www.stevebrakerbooks.com and drop me a line. Or alternatively send me an email and I will add you to the list. My email address is steve@stevebrakerbooks.com I look forward to speaking to you soon.

Copyright

This is a work of fiction. Names, characters, and incidents either are the products of the author's imagination or are used fictitiously and any resemblance to persons, living or dead, businesses, companies, events, is entirely coincidental.

The locations and distances are real, the Area Exists. This is a fictional story based very loosely on the events which took place on November 28th 2002, the Paradise Hotel Bombing in Kikambala Kenya. All information used is freely available on the Internet. The bombing was an actual event. This story in no way corroborates or agrees with any of the theories put forward. There are no allegiances to the hotel or any owners of the hotel past or present.

Copyright © 2017

All rights reserved

Printed in Great Britain
by Amazon